THE
MEDIA MIDAS
BENDING TRUTHS FOR VIRAL WEALTH

SUJAL DAS

outskirts
press

*To each of you who respect truth and science
and refuse to be influenced by envy and vitriol
created daily on social media platforms.*

FOREWORD BY
THE AUTHOR

Einstein's theory of relatively created new conceptions of time. Unscrupulous politicians applied his ground-breaking research to strife and pursuit of power to create highly destructive atom bombs that changed the course of history. A similar phenomenon is occurring in the contemporary world. This time, it is new conceptions of truths or alternative truths created using social media products and technologies. The dichotomy of truths is causing dramatic changes in human behavior and fracturing societies.

Two billion individuals connected using social media platforms are becoming increasingly divided with far left and right views. Lately, Donald J Trump's often reckless but successful use of social media has taken the far-reaching effects of the software platforms to a cataclysmic level. Another six billion are getting primed for new categories of venom and divisions as they get connected the same way. Trump and the creators of these online platforms are setting the course for a new generation of dangerous politicians and dictators.

This book is a fictional novel based on the pursuits of the American businessman and reality TV star. It consists of chapters about places where new conceptions of truths impact the psyche of people differently. Some scenarios may involve exaggerations of true events, and some may be entirely conceived from imagination. The book demonstrates the impact each human being has from variations in truth and affirms Trump's political strategy and rise to power. It takes flight with a study of how Trump is able to bend truths, one at a time, in his favor to win the presidency. Later, unexpected consequences unravel when he attempts to apply the same principles for personal wealth expansion, the fundamental motivation behind his pursuit of the highest office on earth.

The quest by the actor in these vignettes is age-old. The insatiable desire for tremendous fame and wealth underscores each action. But the methods followed are brand new and mind-boggling. Media-driven fame and fortune in the modern world can be achieved quickly. One just needs to be constantly trending or in the news, and the popularity effect goes viral. In an incredible way, the modern mechanics needed for success in the new world fit his seventy-year old nature like a glove.

If only he could use the platform of the most powerful office in the world and apply the same modern mechanics, that would generate the mother of all viral effects. The realization is nothing short of genius. The upshot will be a unique touch that promises tremendous wealth creation. In other words, the modern-day Midas touch.

THE
MEDIA MIDAS

PROLOGUE

The year is 1918. A forty-nine-year-old hardworking father from Queens in New York City has pneumonia-like symptoms and dies in a day.

A year has passed, and his young son continues to be devastated. He is tended by his mother every night in their two-story home in Woodhaven. The darkness brings terrifying nightmares and visions of the future. A vivid dream is forming behind his eyelids while his mother's cool comforting palms gently stroke his face and fevered forehead.

It begins in the dark, medieval alleyways of Gamla Stan in Stockholm. The Spanish Flu is raging through the country's

1

boroughs, counties, villages, and towns. Thirty-five thousand men, women and children have perished.

At a pub in the famous Old Town, smoke from pure Cuban tobacco and the strong smell of local brews hang in the air. One of the patrons is indigenous – a Sami. Standing six feet tall, his handsome face sports a black bushy moustache and a wide forehead with a receding hairline.

The aura of contemporary life and the hums of political debates in the pub percolate into the barbaric, almost ghostly settings outside. Many events begin to unfold in the maze of forgotten courtyards and deserted alleyways. The Sami, infected by the flu, is in a frenzy. He steps out of the pub.

His walk down an empty cobble-stone street is guided by the faint light of a lantern. The past is brought back to life – the smell and taste of medieval Stockholm. Horrifying tales of public executions and unsolved murders lurk in every corner, as do strange myths and legends. But none hits harder than the shocking effects of the Spanish Flu epidemic that has been rampant in the neighborhoods for more than a year.

In the main courtyard, a crowd has begun to gather. These individuals are centrists in their views. There is peace, kindness, and patience in their demeanor. They dress differently, some are short, some are tall, they have different skin colors, some are thin, some are heavy, and there were others who are athletic and muscular. They all look normal and conventional.

Slowly, thick fog accompanied by mist rolls in. On the fringes of the gathering in the courtyard, some individuals begin to forge extreme views of the world. They split away from the centrist group into a rightist group and a leftist group.

The two new groups are restless. The individuals begin to look alike; same size and contour of the foreheads, same bend in their noses, same slant in their eyes, same length and tilt of their eyebrows, same color and flesh in their lips, the same shape of jawline above each neck, same shape of their ears with lobes of the same size. The women have long blonde hair, with matching style and length. The men have short cropped dark hair, pomaded, and brushed back clean, showing their glistening foreheads. These people lose their names and titles.

At the intersection of the centrist, rightist and leftist groups, the people responsible for law enforcement begin to appear. They wear immaculately pressed uniforms; they have badges and identities. And under the shadows of their large hats fixed with black chinstrap and gold buttons, each face is dark.

The conversations among the centrists are audible. They dwell on the food they eat, their children, their work, the places they visit, the schools they had attended, or their children now attend, and markets they visit to buy clothes and vegetables. They never talk about politics, religion, or ideologies.

The rightists and the leftists speak in sign language and use their hands and fingers to communicate what they think are the pressing issues in the country and the best ways to resolve them. Members of the two groups make unsupported claims and assertions relating to politics, religion, ideologies. The approach to solving problems are widely varied. The disagreements are communicated forcefully using the hands and fingers, with all parts of fleshy red faces twitching in anger, but no words are uttered.

The centrists try to mediate without success. Soon, the motion of the hands and fingers turn to shoving and pushing - first among a few individuals in the groups, then rapidly it spills out throughout the courtyard, increasing in intensity. Violence breaks out and many people are injured. Some are killed.

The law enforcers rush in and disperse the mobs. They sternly order the three groups to go back home, vacate the courtyard. No arrests or citations are made because the perpetrators and the victims belong to the leftist and rightist groups who have no identities. With no fear of penalties or jail time for individuals, the two extreme groups find utopia and their membership multiples at a rapid pace.

Loud claps of thunder roll across the dark sky above the church spires before heavy rain begins to lash the cobblestones and trees in the courtyard. As the fog in Gamla Stan rapidly disperses in the deluge, a shocking new society is formed.

The faint light of dawn percolates through the second-floor bedroom window of the modest house in Woodhaven. Soft shapes of shadowy figures begin to emerge, including the pale and tired face of the sixteen-year-old boy. The mother has retired to her side of the bed and is fast asleep. She made a resolve to help her son out with a business. To wean him off the sudden and intense grief. To direct his intelligent mind toward building self-esteem and wealth.

Over the next 70 years, the young boy will build a real estate business, starting from almost nothing and reaching net worth close to a billion dollars. Rather strangely, from the numerous nightmares and haunting visions he had suffered, he develops a knack to see the future. As a result, he is able to achieve many financial windfalls by staying well ahead of others in his business strategies. He knows exactly which cards to play and when to walk away as social and economic circumstances unfold in the country over the decades. He also becomes the still point of his favorite son's recklessly turning world and unimaginable fame.

It is 2020 and another pandemic has ensued. More than two hundred thousand people have perished in the most advanced nation on earth. The course of events at the present is a mirror image of what transpired as an apparition in the mind of the disturbed and grieving young boy from

Queens, almost a century ago. This time however, the devastating effects of the lethal disease are exacerbated by an already deeply divided society with contrarian beliefs.

A political strategist from Los Angeles devised a plan and a recipe six years ago to fracture the country. But he did not foresee the unexpected effects of his intensely planned but twisted scheme.

THE POLITICAL STRATEGIST

With a Master of Arts in national security studies from Georgetown University School of Foreign Service, and a Master of Business Administration degree with honors from Harvard Business School, he is without a doubt highly qualified. He has a calm persona, like still water that runs deep. His thoughts and opinions are often unfathomable. It is 2014 and a jihadist group called ISIL has ruthlessly beheaded two white men, while simultaneously recording and broadcasting the gruesome events over streaming media. He is terribly annoyed by the successful tactics employed by the group to recruit insurgents. He develops a theory that the Western world will soon be under the grip of Islamic fascism. His homeland, in an alarming way, is primed for such an attack.

The straight grey and black strands of hair above his wise forehead are just too dense and stubborn for the gel he has applied; they constantly fall across his face. An uneven stubble stretches all the way from under his sharp but sunken eyes to a prominent chin. His eyes stare at nothing in the deep blue above the Los Angeles skyline as he pulls both his feet up on the desk. Strewn next to his favorite brown suede loafers are heaps of papers with alt-right articles for the newspaper he heads as executive editor.

A yellow colored building houses twelve highly productive reporters with extreme nationalistic views and alliances. It stands bravely at the heart of the widely liberal metropolis. The executive editor's office is modest with large windows, some covered by blinds. On one of them, the theme and spirit of the newspaper #WAR is painted in bold letters. It is a constant reminder that they are members of a fight club, fronting a war against the deep-rooted establishment.

He pulls a marker pen from the holder and begins to rapidly read an article from one of his brightest reporters. He skims through the text rapidly making editorial marks here and there and then suddenly, he stops. He just finished reading a paragraph that details how ISIL influences opinions of insecure and vulnerable men and women across the world using social media. Membership in the group has grown by leaps and bounds in just two years. And each member, once indoctrinated, is a staunch believer in the ideals of the jihadist group. They will stand steadfast to support and honor those ideals. Even to death with no questions asked.

He pulls out his cell phone to call the reporter who wrote the article and asks her to come to his office immediately. She is a sprightly woman in her late thirties, with a law degree from the University of California in Los Angeles. The executive editor always appreciates the precision of her logic in the way she defends her assertions. He attributes the skill to her academic training at the prestigious law school. Professional admiration aside, she however always keeps a safe distance from the thrice divorced sixty-year-old. His most recent wife accused him of alcoholism, antisemitic rants and domestic violence.

She knocks on the door and enters the office gingerly and takes the farthest chair from the desk. The executive editor returns his feet to the floor and stands up.

She knows that her boss has been disturbed for six long years under the presidency of a black man with a Muslim name and a globalist agenda. Under his administration, the jihadist group has made incredible strides, infecting and hurting many deep sections of society. Colored immigrants have taken the reign at many multinational corporations that are foundations of American capitalism. When he points his fingers to sentences in a paragraph she wrote, she begins to ponder why she might have been called to his office, an unusual behavior for the loner.

He sees the path to a new resurrection for his ailing nation. Many cross-sections of the society are frustrated and insecure. The iron is hot, and one needs to strike now to revert the nation back to past greatness. He directs her to open her laptop as he begins to chart a course in his disturbed mind.

For the next hour, the executive editor dictates his ideas; they flow out of his mouth like a river bursting through a dam. The slender fingers of the reporter type feverishly until a six-page report is completed and printed.

The reporter asks if the article should be targeted for the weekend edition. The executive editor smiles for the first time and takes the sheets from her hand. During the next few weeks, he will switch his role and become a political strategist. He just has the right person in mind who can become the next president of the country.

He asks if she will lead the activities of the newspaper while he is away, expecting a nod of affirmation. The ambitious reporter promptly accepts. He assures her emphatically that if his plan is successful, the readership of their newspaper will skyrocket.

He places the sheets carefully in his briefcase and heads out of the office in a haste. He must catch the next direct American Airlines flight to New York city.

As the taxi takes off from his apartment building, he pulls out his phone and begins to type in a few vital notes for himself. The message to the voters will have to be very precise and simple, should hit those strings in their hearts that are hurting the most. The deliverer of the message he has in mind is a controversial figure. This makes him very anxious.

From highway 405, the taxi veers left toward Sepulveda Boulevard and then heads south for approximately ten minutes through downtown Westchester before entering the Los Angeles International Airport. He concludes that many established truths will need to be bent beyond anything one can imagine. Only that will ensure success of his strategy.

THE MOTIVATING TRUTH

The superlatives must be in everything the flamboyant New York businessman is associated with. His excessive love for fame and wealth embodies modern-day royalty. His penthouse at the heart of Manhattan is built in the likeness of the Palace of Versailles and the extravagance of his favorite King Louis XIV. While his energy remains vibrant, he also knows he is getting older and may be quickly losing the touch. He needs a recourse. A final homerun. Badly.

He is in his favorite dark navy-blue suit, a silky white shirt with pure gold cufflinks and a contrasting red striped tie. He leans forward in his chair, hands clasped, toward a powerful TV producer. The young producer in his late thirties notices the businessman's prominent logo on the cufflinks – the first letter of the famous family name. Unlike the older man, he is in casual jeans and a black T-shirt. A well-groomed French beard and a very visible shell necklace dangling loosely from his long neck gives him a subtle but distinct look.

The two have been tycoons in their own worlds of business and entertainment. About seven years ago, they began to collaborate to bring the two worlds and themselves together. The outcome - a hit TV show that has established the businessman as a hero. Over drinks and hors d'oeuvres, the two reminisce their success together.

The primetime show is about an urban jungle and love of money. The backdrop is a supersaturated mosaic of the skyscrapers of Manhattan. Many are studded with the same golden logo as on the businessman's cufflinks. The reflection of clouds speed over the glass surfaces of buildings that shadow the bustling streets below with aggressively moving yellow checker cabs. The hands on all the clocks on many of the building facades move fast to reflect the pace of the city. The names of the businessman and the main cast feature as neon signs like the Wall street tickers, gliding by, as if led by the hands of the clocks. The brilliance of the TV producer projects the numerous bankruptcies and failures of the businessman in a new light. Single handedly, using the sharpness of his brain and negotiating skills, the businessman has fought back and won. The show is about teaching ordinary people hungry for wealth – the cast members – the skills needed to win in the big league.

Like Clint Eastwood of the Wild West, the New York businessman is cast as a true American hero of modern capitalism, the essence of the country's greatness. If one is loyal to the businessman, he will be defended come hell or high water. If not, he shall be vanquished. These are fundamental principles that have enabled the business leaders of the country to create jobs and a wealth base that can support the entire world. The show is a tribute to a culture that has made the country great. The businessman is a posterchild of that much desired ethos.

Fourteen seasons of the successful TV show have passed. The businessman has raked in more than $200M. More importantly, his brand and logo have received a significant boost in value, raising the royalty proceeds from his licensing deals. The Forbes lists the businessman in the top 800 billionaires worldwide with his fortune worth in excess of $3 billion. To the businessman however, being in the top 800 is great but not superlative. It is time for a new gig. He leans forward further toward the TV producer in anticipation as his clasped hands tighten the grip on each other.

The immensely talented producer suggests an idea that is veneered in nothing but grandeur. He plants an imposing image into the businessman's craving mind. It has an unusually hypnotic effect on the businessman. The idea seems like a glorious continuum of the recent success on TV.

Imagine the show now occurring on the rapidly expanding power and reach of social media, the producer continues.

Imagine the actors standing around the Resolute Desk in the Oval Office. The striped tie on his neck rhymes with the nation's flag behind him, as he sits behind the immaculately curved English oak desk, smiling. His staff members, one by one, speak of the great privilege to serve the new president and his political agenda to take the nation to new heights. Just like the contestants in the TV show, they are flabbergasted by his immense talent.

Winning the election may be an uphill task; however, just a successful run for the presidency may suffice, the businessman surmises. His message to the nation, and policies targeted at each individual must create new hope and an unfettered base of fans. Like that of his television audience, the base of supporters is pulled in herds, this time growing more rapidly to a significantly larger scale.

With this new act, the maelstrom of victory and triumph associated with him will be agitated to stunning splendor. His presence in both the traditional and social media would go viral, enhancing his wealth to levels beyond that of King Louis IV, and making his golden touch more prolific than that of King Midas.

THE PLOT AGAINST
THE ELITES

The organist at St. Patrick's Cathedral on New York City's Fifth Avenue is wearing his best suit, ready for the Sunday morning choir. Multiple colors sparkle through the stained-glass panels on Rose Window over the main entrance. The dispersed sunlight adorns the 1879 pipe organ that stands proudly in the altar. This unusually humid August day is just another one to the organist. His fingers meander effortlessly over the stream of black and white keys. The church fills up to the brim with rich sound from the ranks of pipes of differing timbre, pitch, and volume.

A few blocks down, the seventy-two-year-old businessman paces up and down in the living room of his penthouse on the 33rd floor. In a surprising way, despite his six feet tall overweight frame, he is very agile. Unlike the organist, it's a very unique August morning for him.

Stars are beginning to align for him. Eight weeks ago, he experienced a stunning idea, thanks to his favorite TV producer. And just three weeks later, the executive editor-turned-political strategist delivered a theme and recipe to him. He was convinced instantly, as he is normally or never. Over an intense twenty-five minutes, the political strategist prescribed something he believed could win him the presidency of the country. The theme requires him to learn and practice populism and nationalism. The recipe will require him to devise tactics that defeat the policies of the staunch enemy - the elites.

His gold-festooned penthouse is a cocoon that keeps him far removed from everything he considers ordinary. That has, so far, included all forms of populism and nationalism. All his life, he has projected himself as an elite, immensely popular among the rich and powerful. His unusually short fingers on a disproportionately large palm lightly comb his golden hair. His sharp eyes survey the headlines through the polythene wrapping yet to be removed from the Washington Post on the desk. The large TV screens mounted on gold-crowned walls are playing but he isn't paying attention to them. Those screens let reality into his penthouse, but only as rationed by his favorite cable channels. He picks up the Post, removes it from the wrapper, and crumples the pages carelessly under his right arm before he heads to the elevator.

On this unique Sunday morning, a significantly modest West Village apartment on Cornelia Street awaits his arrival. He acquired it two weeks ago, almost in a frenzy. But he did negotiate hard as usual. He was satisfied he got the better end of the bargain.

Large bay windows let in the early afternoon sun. Muddled sounds from Cornelia street below drifts through the room. A full grain leather armchair is perched close to the window with the widest view. His favorite piece of furniture, he insisted it be moved from the penthouse. It creaks slightly as he stretches over to get a sweeping view of the people walking the street. Those are a section of the elites, his enemy.

Bustling cafés line the blocks in the streets of West Village. In many of them on Cornelia street right below the apartment, a group of elites are in deep discussion about the state of the country. Others, alone in their own worlds, are reading books on Kindles. Still some others with dogs are just watching other people, contemplating deep ideas to put to words, probably not related to those people.

Unusually large red roses attract people into the flower shop at the corner of West Fourth and Cornelia Streets. A professor is no exception. He is on his way to meet his fiancé, a ballet dancer and dance teacher. Later, over an espresso and a latte, they sit close, his right arm lovingly around her. They remember her father who died a week ago. He lived in a fishermen community in Winthrop near the Boston harbor. The community perished three years before he did, as lucrative shoals of mackerel and hordes of king crab colonies disappeared rapidly with the rise in the ocean water temperature.

In the same café, a group of doctoral students in international relations argue and lament at the demise of concerted efforts by the north and south American nations to eliminate the drug cartels of Mexico and Columbia. One of them has been severely hurt by the recent overdose of his favorite nephew. A mother loses her train of thought as she pulls the collar on her distracted dog. Another disturbing story of women sexually harassed at work is taking shape on her MacBook.

The elites of West Village, and specifically those on Cornelia where his apartment stands unceremoniously, live off truths. Founded in deep science, literature, and the arts, they go squarely and precisely against the grain of the prescribed rightwing theme and recipe. Therefore, they must be first understood and then debunked.

As the evening progresses to late night, deeper truths, science, and facts emerge in the dimmer lights and louder discussions. They underpin the positive impacts of globalization. Under a large masquerading hat, the businessman's eyes and nose twitch. The overwhelmingly contrarian theme by the rightwing strategist excites him: globalism is at the root of all decline; the elites are controlling and comfortable managing that decline.

The lights and sounds from the outside fade to nothing as dawn covers West Village. The pitch darkness and still-ness in the room further intensifies the feverish pace of his thoughts. The armchair creaks even louder as his heavy frame shifts uncomfortably. Ideas emerge with the fury of lava and solidify rapidly as they hit the cold steeliness of his fierce ambition.

The truths of the elites must be bent.

He needs a new world where people suffer from short atten-tion spans. Time must assume a new dimension. It becomes significantly disjointed and moves faster than ever before. What is perceived as truth evolves over those fragments of time, and often changes to the opposite.

The truths of the elites must be bent, he repeats.

He needs a new world where people lose their localism. Space must take on an all-expansive new dimension where physical proximity has no meaning. Ideas and opinions can be casually hurled across as truths over long distances with-out the need or responsibility to defend.

The disjointed nature of time, compounded by the loss of proximity and responsibility, makes truths highly malleable. Each truth can now have two sides. One side can be per-ceived as the fact and the other as an alternative fact, con-ceived for selfish gains.

Over the next several months, the businessman remains veiled as a local of West Village and stays close to the enemy. Assisted closely by the political strategist, he develops many ideas to undermine the truths of the elites. Each idea will play on the very soul of the nation. They will be applied to cross sections of the society across the length and breadth of the country.

TRUTHS AS SIMPLE, SHORT BURSTS

The beard on his wrinkled, chubby cheeks and chin need a trim. The bags under his eyes are sagging more than usual. The political strategist has not slept many nights. The effect of Hitler's Nuremberg Rally must be repeated constantly. Daily if possible, he reiterates to the media savvy businessman.

Simple ideas are easier to grasp; they usher in hope easily. Especially in times of trouble. It is also easier to slip in propaganda in such ideas. The gradient from simplicity to propaganda that treacherously begins to divide people is hard to assess. Hitler's message in the 1930s was simple; it caught the attention and admiration of the German masses when economic woes lurched in every corner of their lives. Nazism emerged almost naturally and became pervasive. The shifts to intense racial divisions and gross cruelty, as fostered by Hitler's simple but forceful messages, occurred almost naturally.

The strategist opens his laptop and logs into his social media account. He emphasizes to the businessman how this wildly popular software platform forces simplicity of communication by limiting the author's thoughts and characters to a parsimonious count of 140. This pervasive medium can propagate ideas very quickly which stick in people's minds like hard-to-remove glue. The businessman logs in himself, swipes his thumb on his iPhone as features of the software application get revealed. With that, his own future as the president of the country. Only if he can amplify the anguishes of the people.

In this platform, new ideas, layered with attractive tints of controversy, can be communicated in short bursts. The simple message can empower one instance of the world to shun the undesirable present and trajectory of the future, and recoil back to past glory. Backed by an effective dose of pleasant nostalgia, the ideas can easily elevate to truths.

For example, his simple statements must depict bleak pictures of the dilapidated coal and steel factories in the Rust Belt. Inside them, in foggy darkness, he will magnify images of the destruction of common men and women by the elites. He must carefully balance what he says, maintain the tilt safely toward simplicity, add a lie or two, but never allow any hint of propaganda.

For the most part, people care about their daily lives and rightfully so. The perception of ideas by their intent minds is influenced by their genuine aspirations. The businessman must mine this opportunity.

A middle-aged woman and caring mother of two boys drives a Cadillac through a Rust Belt town. The intricately polished vehicle glides by familiar neighborhoods lined with empty and decaying large homes. Memories of the once flourishing liveliness that brightened the lush green yards and sidewalks of Youngstown engulf her. The magical sights of snow-white puppies running past ecstatic children are fresh in her mind. The tall brawny men from those homes, like her husband, worked in the world's leading manufacturing plants that built the fastest cars, and produced the hottest coal and strongest steel. To her and everyone she knows in her town, a promise of the revival of the manufacturing industry is more than music to their ears. It is a miracle that is possible, only if the powerful might of their country is put to proper use.

In another part of the town, at the University, a young white student shudders to log into his social media pages, fearing posts about more deaths of his friends, from overdose. One of them, a twenty-eight-year-old graduate who loved mathematics was found dead with a needle in his arm. Opioids, some rumored to kill just on touch, permeate every vein of society, in the inner city and upscale suburbs. To the grieving relatives and friends, the free flow of opioids is tantamount to invasion of their daily lives. The bright young student, like most others at the University, concludes that stopping this invasion at all costs is paramount.

In the east side of Youngstown, many thoughtful minds collectively work hard on pages of history books and web sites in the library. The historic institution, housed in a majestic Victorian style building, overlooks the Mahoning River. The thoughtful gazes through cathedral style glass panes to neighborhoods across the river are mindful of the growing unemployment and the decline of the precious community spirit. Their intense research centers on precedence, specifically the historical incidents where misguided policies drove flourishing, powerful civilizations to decay.

A compelling illustration of how history could repeat itself is the fall of the Roman Empire. The emperors' policies led to devastating effects that bear stark resemblances to contemporary debacles in society. In an eerie way, the once insurmountable glory of their country is now showing signs of faltering.

Rome's borders expanded in all directions with annexation of adjacent countries. The empire ran out of people to guard the borders. There weren't enough Romans, so they let others in. Strong and barbaric people from foreign lands turned out to be perfect guardians. Initially, their presence was constrained to only the periphery of society. Their unfamiliar religion and culture did not matter. Later, leveraging and sometimes misusing lenient policies, the aliens infiltrated into the heart of Roman society. The foundational discipline and coherent culture of the original people began to dilute. With that came the eventual decline and fall of the empire itself.

The researchers at the library in Youngstown conclude that local interests should override globalist expansion by all means.

Jobs, safety, and vitality of the society they live in are most important to the people in this cross section of society. Intense aspirations for a better life in these communities create an attractively ripe situation. It invites precise strikes to break the status quo. These forays are simple ideas that are very sticky, thanks to their controversial nature and tints of falsehood. They can spread virally on the 140-character social media platform. The businessman revels in many bright approaches that can lead him to victory.

To start with, jobs and past glory related to the steel and coal industries can be miraculously brought back to the people. An effortless placement of big enough tariffs is all that is needed. Rogue nations that have been stealing manufacturing jobs will be turned on their heels.

Next, a tall and continuous concrete wall along the southern border will stop the invasion of drugs like crystal methamphetamine from the Latin American countries. The surplus of steel manufactured with the return of the industry back into local neighborhoods is used to build an even stronger wall.

Finally, globalism can be brought to a screeching halt to preserve precious local identity and resources. Cultural dilution fostered by unchecked immigration is eliminated. A ban on the movement of the most dangerous religious and ethnic groups through the country's ports of entry is proclaimed. Similarly, the incessant draining of precious resources to issues like climate change and foreign wars that pertain to other countries is abruptly stopped.

Many truths will be hidden or ignored in such communication and implementation of policies. The sophistication of many realities will be conveniently left out – such as the effects of new technologies and related skill, the significant difference in wages across borders, the smuggling of drugs through legal ports of entry and the negative impacts of climate change. Surprisingly, the blatant masking of these facts with subtle lies will only give the businessman's words significantly faster tailwind. His comforting and easily graspable ideas will spread virally.

The elites, on the other hand, in an expected and somewhat dull way, will discount the above policies as unimplementable, and their justification as propaganda based on falsehoods. The detailed discourses and research reports that prove their points will not matter. They are just too long and complex for the common people. As a result, the elites' approaches are equated to sheer insensitivity to the needs of the common people. As headwinds, such perceptions further stall the propagation of their ideas. The pride in their deep intellect and complicated facts become their Achilles' heel. Because, the common people, unlike the elites, accept the much simpler and controversial ideas as a breath of fresh air, a surer path of return to past glory, a revival of precious identity.

As a result, such ideas, communicated within the bounds of intellect possible in 140 characters, will become truths.

Donald J. Trump ✔
@realDonaldTrump

How amazing, the State Health Director who verified copies of Obama's "birth certificate" died in plane crash today. All others lived

TESTS OF TRUTH
CIRCUMVENTED

There are many tests of truths, proven and accepted over the ages. However, an opinion or impression presented in a certain form or by an individual of certain stature may not be subject to such tests of truth. It is accepted without opposition and immediately becomes a truth.

The sight of the art deco buildings spanning the 5th and 6th Avenues always gets his spirits up. The cold winter wind plays with the checked blue scarf around his neck as the reporter slides past the sparkling automatic glass doors of Rockefeller Center. The fitted gloves tightly grip the matching leather backpack that holds his laptop. In it is an eleven-page investigative report. Only this morning as he typed anxiously, many disjoint pieces of the report that he has been diligently preparing for many weeks finally came together to take shape. The publication he is writing for will question every claim and conclusion. They will be tested for truth and strict conformance to ethics in journalism. As his polished black shoes step into the elevator, his mind checks off the foundation of truth in each revelation in the report. As if, each check mark is on a trait of his own character.

On the blood red mahogany desk in the chief editor's office, each precious word in the investigative report is laid bare. As naked facts, the assertions expressed must stand purely on their own merit. The editor's forty years of experience in the field built on a doctorate from Harvard bestows her significant authority. The facts pass through each test of intellectual authority. Next, all pertinent facts are arranged in a consistent and cohesive fashion as an integrated whole. Where arts and sciences are applicable, formal logic and mathematical rules are applied as tests of rigorous consistency. When aspects of personal morality and social behavior are in question, a statistical method such as majority rule of accepting assertions and proposals is applied. By late afternoon, the facts in the report, each considered as ordinary and unembellished - without any tint of emotion, instinct or prior belief – pass each test of truth and is approved for publication the next morning.

The discussions, thoughts, ideas, revelations, and claims expressed in the cafés of West Village aren't much different. Behind the gold-inscribed floral drapes of the apartment above Cornelia Street, the ideas conceived are however, very different. At the core, they are bare. Adorned and etched exquisitely like ornaments, they are then preordained to be extraordinary and harbingers of great hope. The facts in this world of the common people are elevated and grand with precious ideologies and identities hemmed into them. Tests of truth do not apply to them.

The nurse at Lehigh Valley Hospital is on a break. Fall colors laden on richly canopied trees in the compound set the distant blue Allentown sky on fire. The pensive stare sharpens as his attention returns to matters in his proximity. The next round of patients gathering in front of the receptionist receives a distant but intense assessment. His experience has trained him to prejudge ailments and predict potential care. He learned the importance of preparedness and diligence from his grandfather who worked his way up from digging iron ore to becoming an executive in a pig iron production company.

His father dived into severe depression after the manufacturing company that employed him shut down. The once strong and always-smiling dad committed suicide when he was only four years old. Unlike his grandfather, the nurse knows that his level of success working in the service industry will never be spectacular. At the bar in the street corner by his grandfather's colonial-style house, every evening over whiskey, he talks or dreams of a fictitious father figure.

Having achieved astonishing success with brick and mortar, iron and steel, media and television, the father of his dreams is a billionaire and a star. The nurse wants to lean on that reassuring shoulder and listen to firm assertions that the might and competency of the manufacturing industry in Allentown will be resurrected - to be the biggest and the greatest and the most spectacular.

There are many people like the nurse. The stardom and prosperity of the father-figure project on the brave aspirations of the community. The tall assurances from the father-figure are soothing. Communicated in hyperbole, the pledges raise the world of these people to a higher state of being. The aspirations then become definitive as achievable truths.

The Presbyterian Church perched off route 96 in the west end of Wichita can easily go unnoticed. The meticulous design of the ivory reredos inside has always been a source of pride to the pastor. In contrast, he has always despised the almost flat design of the dome above it. A middle-aged man whose parents migrated from a small village in Italy, he is also an architecture major.

Every Sunday morning, he completely relinquishes his artistic views. Top of mind to him and his followers at the church is the Bible as the ultimate moral and historical authority.

Silhouettes of groups of new families appear, blocking the blinding sunlight otherwise gushing in through the main church door. Their brown skin and pitch-black hair emerge distinctly as they take seats in the pew. Anxious to mingle and appear normal, they quickly lean forward into the kneelers, ready to absorb the pastor's sermons.

People of other faiths or non-believers of the supreme faith must be christened, and this warrants a new order. The pastor calls on his followers to evangelize and spread the faith. So that those that are faithless or are of an unknown faith can be born again. Across the country, a pervasive effect can be achieved only if the government and the judicial systems are on the side of the evangelicals.

If the top officials in the government and new appointees into the judicial system are evangelicals, and the moral code as defined by the Bible becomes the core of the country's jurisprudence, the entirety of the nation can be born again, can be great again.

Many traits of the businessman in the apartment on Cornelia Street are immoral. On the pretext of being a celebrity, he has taken many liberties. As weapons that can be easily wielded by his enemy, these past transgressions can destroy his prospects of winning the presidency.

Accepting mistakes and apologies are not part of his playbook. Deflection and persistent denials are. The businessman must stitch in strong ideology so that all truths pertaining to scandals and immoral behavior become irrelevant.

Even David, who took down Goliath, had a decadent past, yet God chose him. Immoral traits of the businessman standing on a God-centered, Biblical agenda must be forgiven.

False denials or deflections of past immoral behavior must be ingeniously correlated to the religious identity of the people and become accepted as truths.

The distinct sound of Nancy Sinatra from the nineties vintage CD player reverberates around the makeshift workshop in the garage.

"...now he's gone, I don't know why...and 'till this day, sometimes I cry...he didn't even say goodbye...he didn't take the time to lie...bang bang, he shot me down...bang bang, I hit the ground...bang bang, that awful sound..."

The Chevy car mechanic nods the synergy of his life to the song as he runs the copper bore brush in and out, polishing the inside of the barrel of his automatic rifle. His childhood sweetheart quietly drifted away from his life like a log of wood on gentle water. At some point in their lives, he was just done with her, plain and simple. Emotions and lies were never at play.

In his garage workshop, the Texan pride, the no nonsense attitude, and the love of guns live in perfect harmony. The muzzle of the AR-15 rifle manufactured by Runner Guns at Eagle Gun Range in Lewisville feels just right in his firm grip. His heavyset wife yells from the backyard as the bar-beque beef steak loses simmer, waiting on a plate topped with his favorite black beans on the side. The checkered red shirt under his tattered blue denim jacket soaks in a few drops of sweat from his forehead. This is another hot Sutherland Springs afternoon.

The South and East of Highway 87 protects the remnants of past glory of a hundred Sulphur springs. The identity of the original inhabitants of Old Town is distinct. Immigrants encroach on their town, jobs, and livelihood. Still, like the cast iron ornamentation around the vault door of the roof-less former bank building, their pride remains intact.

Overzealous news casters on television channels and fake bots on social media exacerbate the threat of assaults on the people. The attacks are not only on their professions, but also on their daughters and wives, synonymous to rape.

The inhabitants decry "there are no more safe places in our world". So, they bring their guns to church on Sunday and to the office on Monday. Students carry them on the college campus, so do the foremen at the construction site and the Chevy car mechanic at his workshop. They carry them in their cars and on their boats.

The belief in the right to own guns is the foundation of this community's true identity. The elites and their governments conspire to confiscate their guns under the false pretext of safer neighborhoods. The torrent of sensational news firmly establishes an indelible paranoia; the fear of loss of precious identity converts the bulletins, broadcasts, and reports into de facto truths.

In the world comprising the communities of Allentown, Wichita and Sutherland Springs, the tests of truth can be circumvented using the powers of fame, ideology, and identity. Espousing deep knowhow about contemporary global forces, pure science and indelible learnings from historical events, the elites of West Village discount this theory. They sadly disregard the deep social and financial wounds suffered by the ingenuous people of these communities.

The businessman in the apartment on Cornelia Street is further emboldened. He obsessively scrubs the already clean glass panes of the bay window, looks down and smiles at their intellectual arrogance.

ILLUSORY TRUTHS

The businessman needs a new persona. He needs an alternate world like he created in the hit primetime TV show.

The greatness of the nation has been compromised. The future is bleak. Many infusions of deep conspiracies that caused the debacle are brewing in his mind. The world must change the current forward course because any hope of a new utopia can only be found in the past.

He must create a new concoction of fantasy with relentless repetitions. These will be illusory truths. They will manifest as another set of alternative facts.

The new truths will have to be delivered effectively to the

people while building a façade of his own persona. Will he be able to establish their validity? Will they stick long enough during the course of the campaign, and the following four long years of the first term of his presidency?

⊗⊗⊗

On this crisp fall morning, a magician consumes a hearty eggs benedict breakfast in a café on Greenwich Street in West Village. He has walked all the way from the far west side where the Meatpacking District is. His abhorrence of the snobbishness of Las Vegas, where he resides, exacerbated as he walked the unique grid of streets. The refreshing urban bohemian atmosphere that emerged from each intersection lifted his spirits.

In contrast to how he excels in his profession, everything feels so authentic. A psychology major, he could never make ends meet working on his patients' minds by applying science. His other innate talent - the sleight of hand – also plays on peoples' minds but is a far cry from any form of science. This profession, however, has been a resounding commercial success. He leaves a hefty tip for the ever smiling and petite waitress and steps out of the café.

With thoughtful eyes fixed at the distant front, he walks hastily toward Cornelia Street. He adjusts his tie and brushes any leftover lint on his coat. He is underwhelmed by the modest front porch of the apartment. As he climbs up the steps, he is expecting quite the opposite when he meets the businessman known for his flamboyance.

The tall white entry door opens. And it begins to play out as he had imagined - a very generous and welcoming grin complemented by a warm and soft handshake. In the brightly lit living room with rich marble floors, the magician and the businessman sit across an oversized coffee table with ornate brass borders. The butler serves Turkish coffee to the psychology major and magician, and diet coke with ice in a gold-rimmed glass to the businessman. Over two hours, they discuss how the psychology of repetition works in human brains, and how a magician's art makes lies stick.

There are fewer than ten adults with a bachelor's degree or higher in Atkinson county, Georgia. The plaster-and-stucco contractor is one of them. His four-wheel-drive Ford truck roars through muddy roads; a sizeable portion of the southern county is rural farmland. With programmed dexterity, he maneuvers the truck on a sharp turn that leads to the sprawling parking lot of one of the large employers in the county.

A maker of prefabricated buildings and decorative moldings, the company also employs many of his colleagues who are of Mexican descent. About a quarter of the population in Atkinson are Hispanics and growing. Some of them may be his evening bar mates, but he always questions their eligibility for modestly well-paying jobs like the one he has.

Later that evening at the popular Poole's Pub on Main Street, he huddles closer to white friends and family members. The large television screens continuously flash breaking news about impending voter fraud. The threat in the approaching election is clear - illegal immigrants are being recklessly let into electoral roles in the name of equality and humanity. Their votes can only further policies pushed by the elites and are detrimental to the country. This must be stopped. Voter turnout among the whites is more crucial than ever to ensure those policies are defeated.

The news about voter fraud goes rampant. They are heard loud and clear by everyone in the county, every evening in every bar, grocery, and convenient store, at the bus station, in the barns of all farms and around the offices of government buildings and corridors of schools.

The idea of systemic voter fraud, instigated by the elites of the country, begins to seep into people's heads. The pervasive effect of continuous repetitions in the media clouds their brains. They lose the ability to question the validity of what they hear.

The whitewashed lone house on a lush green hill in Grundy, Virginia reflects a contrasting florescent blue in the pristine moonlight. Inside, a lifelong resident of Buchanan County and a barber for close to 40 years, prepares to go to bed.

At Frank's Barber Shop, situated downtown in this coal

mining town of Appalachia, the profile of her clientele has changed over the years, as if keeping up with the spreading grayness in her hair. Most that come for a trim are older now; the younger ones are leaving for jobs elsewhere.

She and most of her clients do not trust the politicians that make regular trips down from the country's capital to pacify a shrinking town. They all agree that while it is the best place to live, people in Buchanan County need a change. They need a new leader who is different from the current untrustworthy herd. Someone who stands for the forgotten, a voice that does not sound political and speaks only from the heart or from deep conviction.

Opulent hotel and apartment towers that bear the businessman's name and logo prominently appear repeatedly on television advertisements. In the silhouette of one large metropolis after another, across the world. Only the hugely successful businessman has the grit to oppose the herd. By distinctly separating himself from those that cannot be trusted, his assertions and beliefs start to stick in the people's minds. They become truths and in the process he a savior.

The wolf moon over farm buildings in Olin, Iowa lights up the snow on barn roofs. Stacks of hay and firewood line the walls. The forty-five-year-old farmer likes to call himself an entrepreneur. He crosses the freezing barnyard, inspecting portions of his sprawling corn and soybean operation.

A prolific reader, his concern about intellectual property theft by China – whether technology for iPhones or seed genetics – knows no bounds.

China must be taught a lesson – there is consensus among the close-knit Iowa community he influences every Sunday morning at church congregations. Equally concerning to them, however, is the quality of the field of candidates for presidency. They all seem to succumb to the current trading dependencies and deficits with the Asian powerhouse.

Personally, the farmer sees a likeness with the businessman and leans toward him. He is the only one touting tariffs against China. However, the moral flaws in his character are fatal. They are against the doctrines that the minister teaches, and the community follows to each letter.

Over the next several weeks, the news and social media channels are bombarded with news about many thousands of hidden emails by a leading candidate that lay out a conspiracy to kill local coal and textile industries to further a globalist agenda.

The flashy diversion, whether true or false, engages even the most politically apathetic. A fortnight passes by, the moon is now barely visible. The community of Olin, hell bent on teaching China a lesson and dead against globalism, makes up its mind.

Neighbors in Fall River, Massachusetts, gather at Darrell's Diner to debate the politics of the day. Arguments between the dueling tables get heated. The Spindle City of the past was filled with mills producing cotton print cloth. Voices from one table loudly affirm the catastrophic trade deals with neighboring countries while the other seek out proof in real economic data. But all of them agree that the migrants from the south of the border are taking their jobs.

In the weeks to follow, the pain of losing their affluent livelihood of the past reinforce the strong resentment against the migrants. As social media posts and rightwing podcasts repeatedly associate them to crime and drugs, the arguments on the tables subside. Instead, there is unison and cohesive actions that support a simple and precise solution – a wall along the southern border will stop the epidemic for good.

A new reality begins to emerge in the apartment on Cornelia Street. The tall magician's hat gifted to the businessman by his guest stands prominently on the coffee table. His elitist and troublesome records of the past begin to fade into the backdrop. The psychology of repetitions combined craftily with flashy diversions and lies create magic. He becomes the tribune of change.

TRUTHS FOR THE GREATER GOOD

Many threats hang eerily over the greatest nation on earth. Unconventional and least understood, they are critically troublesome.

Fought at each farmer and industrial worker's household, and increasingly on a mass scale in the minds of potentially every citizen, the new wars are more widespread than ever. The enemies' agenda of subtle but sure destruction is becoming imminent. The foreign schemes are proliferated by influencing opinions, one individual at a time, using social media.

In this new threat paradigm, top secret policies are needed

to protect the homeland. These secrets belong to the top brass only. The common people, prone to succumbing to the foreign evil coercions, are kept in the dark using misinformation. In the interest of the greater good, those deflections can be accepted as truths.

The city of Palo Alto in Silicon Valley deliberately maintains an old town look and feel. With sprawling lush green parks and narrow two-lane streets lined with mature oak, eucalyptus and California pepper trees, the charming city is home to the richest corporate executives. Their companies, by constantly advancing the technology landscape, have shaped modern lives worldwide.

The tallest trees touch the old and sagging power lines that crisscross the sky. Under them, the busy sidewalks are strewn with many elderly pedestrians, young joggers, and loving mothers with children in strollers. Rows of multi-million-dollar homes hide behind the ordinary casual demeanor of the town. Keeping in tune with everything else, these properties also lack outright grandeur; they can barely pass as modest looking mansions. A sixty-five-year-old retired executive is a proud resident of one such home that is distinctly French Tudor style.

Ten years back, a massive stroke stole both his voice and the opportunity to be the CEO of one of the most powerful software companies in the world. Fit as an athlete, his passion for rowing has helped him recover physically and mentally. His voice has returned; however, the speech is slow and slurred, preventing a full time return to the corporate world. His close friend and the current CEO of a large hardware company has joined him this morning on their routine brisk walk to the Eleanor Pardee Park. In low hushed voices, they discuss top secret topics straight out of the Pentagon.

The retired executive and his wife are both immigrants. As a smart but impatient engineer and later an aggressive sales account manager, he rose the ranks in the software company while in Denmark. His tall wife takes great pride of her high school basketball team in Shanghai, never missing an opportunity to boast about the athleticism and dexterity of the strong women teammates. At University of California in Berkeley where she studied economics and business, between missing her family in China and adjusting to a new culture, she reluctantly gave up her favorite sport.

The successful couple have been empty nested for almost a decade now; their two children are settled with well-paying jobs and happy families. They had just completed renovating a portion of their home and were wondering what next when one evening, they received a call from the apartment in West Village. Both of them spoke and listened intently to the businessman at the other end of the line. When they hung up, they looked at each other and knew instantly that their lives were about to enter an exciting next chapter.

A job in finance at the businessman's construction company

was a stupendous achievement for the Chinese immigrant. Later, she had the enviable opportunity to work closely with the businessman on one of his most ambitious projects in Atlantic City. After she married the rising star executive at the software company and moved to California, the businessman kept in touch with her.

The call from West Village was an opportunity to relive that past, but this time also with her husband who would advise the presidential candidate on trade and technology-related policies. The experience of the retired executive is considerably valuable because he had led the software company's China operations for more than five years while stationed in Beijing.

A detour through University Avenue is a preferred path to the Eleanor Pardee Park; the two executives prefer to skip the many possible shortcuts through neighborhood streets. The unique and positive vibe on the avenue that leads to Stanford University is known to spawn productive creativity, raise the entrepreneurial spirit in everyone. They walk past the popular cafés and step into an inconspicuous alleyway, toward a mom-and-pop shop situated right on the cul-de-sac. The experienced barista who also owns the rundown café greets the two regular customers and prepares their favorite cappuccino blends without a prompt.

The rich Brazilian coffee invigorates the conversation which soon takes a serious turn as the two executives pace out of the alleyway.

The world has changed; the nation now needs to consider creative paths to remain the leader on all fronts as it has been so far. The confrontations with terrorists and the resulting foreign wars in multiple countries are conventional strategies. Such tactics are quite unlike how the startups of Silicon Valley operate and succeed. They should be forward thinking and different. Only newfound innovations can be effective in the quest to beat competing countries.

The nation must relinquish conventional methods of identifying and dealing with the enemy; it should immediately drop all responsibilities pertaining to conformist and predictable war games. Budgets and resources must be freed up and reallocated. Traditional wars on terrorists must now be fought only as proxy by other nations. Dictatorial regimes are best known to match the evil paths of terrorists and beat them in their own games. They must be incentivized to take on and fight the prolonged wars that have already caused immense casualties. As a result, some members of the long-defined axis-of-evil nations will need to be elevated to friendly, cooperative leaders and governments.

The verdant spread of the tree canopies in Eleanor Pardee Park provides a daylong pleasant ambience on the walkways, bike paths and playgrounds. The locals of Palo Alto and their dogs of all breeds and sizes mingle generously, like one big family. On this cool late-October morning, the brisk stride and intense dialogue keep the two executives completely oblivious of their surroundings. Their tone shift to a hush as they move past groups of chattering locals, reverting back to normal volume only in the most secluded areas under tall redwoods or by the softly flowing creek.

The greatest threat to their nation is from countries that fall in two groups.

Countries in the first group are advancing economically and technologically at a faster pace and can soon surpass the greatest nation on earth. They must be defeated with new trade policies.

Slowing down the pace of progress and productivity in the most advanced nation is the primary goal of the second group of countries. These countries find ways to smuggle in cheap labor, criminals, and drugs to the vulnerable pockets of society. As a result, communities are destroyed, and jobs are stolen. Morals preached by respected pastors during Sunday church gatherings, and by devoted evangelicals at each doorstep of neighborhood households are compromised. The devious intent of these countries must be defeated with stricter border control and immigration policies.

These two groups of countries now form the new axis of evil. The new unconventional wars will need to be fought with advanced and entrepreneurial trade and immigration policies that catch the enemy nations by surprise.

As the morning turns to midday, the two decide to take a break. They sit down on a bench; the refreshingly cool bay breeze begins to dry up the sweat on their foreheads and the backs of their shirts. The retired executive has been asked to draft ideas and proposals that will eventually form the cornerstone of the prospective new president's policies on three fronts. He runs his ideas with the CEO. Both are adept at developing and executing new and unique strategies in companies. When implemented judiciously with skilled personnel, they change the trajectory of company revenue and shareholder value. The magnitude of scope of his ideas this morning is much larger. They are designed to bring back world domination of his nation in a way that will last many generations to come.

First, an effective mix of dictators and regimes must be incentivized to fight the proxy wars against the terrorists on behalf of his nation. On his list are three of them – Russia, North Korea, and Turkey.

Second, he sets his sight on China and Germany as two countries benefiting unfairly from trade policies. They must be slowed down.

Finally, he lists Mexico and many Muslim nations, and their refugees and asylum seekers as countries affecting vulnerable communities and slowing progress.

The CEO interjects with a confused mix of discomfort and hope in his intelligent eyes.

He highlights a list of significant conflicts that will arise.

The new policies will create many controversies by blatantly contradicting well-established and recognized research data from the academia and political experts. Judicial posturing needed to defend the policies will be challenging, bordering on violating the Constitution itself. Impact of widespread negative media and press coverage due to the controversial nature of proposed policy changes can also be crippling. Racial profiling and aggressive positions that go against the grain of well-tested and proven democratic principles will raise massive waves of discord. After all, the nation has been a proud flag bearer of these values since the end of World War I.

Conflicts aside, the CEO emphatically agrees that such policy changes - if successfully implemented - can change the trajectory of the future in the nation's favor. He recommends that the controversial drivers and rationale behind these new policies must remain top secrets. This strategy can help minimize the impact of the potentially paralyzing conflicts. Any undesired side effects of implementing the novel policies and from possible leaks of top secrets will have to be dealt with ingenious deflections.

Later that evening, in the living room of the French Tudor home on Hamilton Avenue, the retired executive and his wife sip an expensive flavor of Zinfandel from a close friend's vineyard. They sit next to each other in the comforting light of the antique stained brass desk lamp on the study table, holding hands. Their eyes are fixated on a three-legged sketch on a clean sheet of paper and at the precious scribblings at the end of each leg.

The letters under each leg start with the heading – top secret, all in upper case. The two proud naturalized citizens are steadfast on the need for the new policies they have devised, however controversial they may be. She wields the black sketch pen in her hand to add a body and a face above the three legs. This unexpected act pleasantly surprises her husband. Next to the face, she jots down three new words – deflections, alternative facts, and mouthpieces. She jokingly adds an orange colored wig above the incomplete face.

It is past midnight in West Village when the cell phone on the dining table both rings and vibrates. It gets the needed attention, the noise somehow surpassing late-night TV blasting on his fresh attentive face. This is a call the businessman does not want to miss.

The voice on the other end speaks slowly and convincingly. The execution strategy has been defined and put in place. The secrets will need to be staunchly protected using deflections and alternative facts. The effective mouthpieces will be the right-wing media compounded by the businessman's tweets and rally speeches riding on his unique instantaneous and apolitical nature.

TRUTH IS PLURALISTIC

The United Boeing 777-200 braves the unsettled April weather and makes a smooth landing at Newark Airport in New Jersey. The couple in their late thirties applaud the pilot with the fellow passengers. They are just about to wrap up their trip to Antarctica.

Fourteen days ago, on their way to the Chilean Villa Las Estrellas base situated off the western tip of the Antarctic Peninsula, they took a break in Rio de Janeiro before embarking on a cruise ship toward the South Pole. The multi-story cruise liner moved fast, pushed by a favorable polar jet stream and in the company of a thousand dolphins and seagulls, through pristine blue waters of late spring.

Once anchored, small boats descended from the topmost

deck of the tall ship into the choppy sea waters; they took the passengers including the couple closer to the southern tip of the earth.

The boats were able to veer unusually close to the South Pole, with melting glaciers opening the ocean further than known in history. On boats and kayaks, they ventured into many iceberg-flanked passageways, into canals of water in between sheets of thick ice out in the open ocean. They watched polar bears wait patiently for the next unfortunate young walrus, and sea gulls fly above them as if inspecting every move.

On the icy shores, they walked with friendly penguins toward Port Lockroy, a former British research station turned museum. There, with locals and other travelers and over beer and hot chocolate, they joined impassioned discussions about the state of nature and wildlife in the South Pole.

Thankfully it is still a virtually uninhabited, unadulterated landmass. But it is being impacted by the irresponsible living habits of humans all across the world. Even the most advanced nations like the one the young couple is from.

Upgraded to business class on their flight back, they relished the wider, comfortable seating, but mostly utilized the more private space to debate and argue their favorite topic – climate change and global warming. It is the reason the working couple planned the unique destination months in advance and artfully convinced their managers at work to allow two weeks off their otherwise busy schedules.

In their arguments, the social worker wife cites data from numerous studies to defend the occurrence of climate change and the dangerous consequences to wildlife and health. The technocrat husband, in contrast, uses the term global warming and debates in earnest that it is a hoax. He emphasizes that time and money the nation spends on global warming amounts to lack of concern for the poor and the immediate challenges facing the middle class in the country.

The healthy dispute ends only when they reach home, change into comfortable pajamas, and open up their respective laptops.

To catchup with events at work, they entrench themselves in the contents of a long list of backed-up emails. They must accomplish this rigor before hitting the bed for undisturbed sleep.

Used synonymously in many conversations, the terms climate change and global warming may convey the same meanings. But they stand on different sets of truths. And they are pluralistic truths, summed up from multiple facts.

Fact #1: The national priority must be to take care of the poor, those affected by the unchecked influx of drugs, and the loss of jobs by the middle class, especially in the Rust Belt. Diverting federal and state budgets away from these simple straightforward needs of the society is nothing short of being belligerent.

Fact #2: There are foreign countries that gain when manufacturing in the home country becomes non-competitive. Any category of globalist agenda only fosters movement of jobs offshore.

Fact #3: The end of the cold war took away a global enemy – the Soviet Union, creating the need for a new one, maybe even a fake one like global warming; the intent being to introduce world government of a second kind.

The above three facts, when summed up, can be used to soundly infer that global warming is a far-fetched idea, even a hoax created for political reasons. This becomes the truth among one set of believers in one world.

Just like Newton's laws of motion, climate change has been established as a real and current phenomenon by well-known scientists. There is a vast amount of statistical data proving that many undesirable changes occurring in the environment will only continue and worsen over time.

Fact #1: The rise in sea levels due to melting of ice is clearly measurable and visible to anyone paying attention.

Fact #2: The marked increases in the intensity of natural calamities like devastating floods, protracted periods of droughts, and raging wildfires worldwide are easily noticeable.

Fact #3: This one is more easily understood by the scientific community - the erosion of the protective layers in the atmosphere against harmful rays. This is caused by the uncontrolled emission of carbon from factories and exponential growth in the number of automobiles in use, especially in developing countries. The effect of pollution and the adverse effects on the health of humans is felt daily in the most populated cities of the world.

To another set of believers in another world, the sum of the above three science-driven facts establishes climate change as the most significant global threat for the current and next generation of humans.

Both worlds exist with the conflicting narratives concerning global warming and climate change. They are valid depending on the vantage point. They cannot be discounted.

And like the couple fast asleep finally at 2 am on a Monday morning under the crisp silver moonlight shining through their bedroom window, individuals from all walks of life can latch on to one or the other way of dissecting this topic – one that impacts daily lives of the common people and one that impacts mother earth.

At an esteemed University campus on the East Coast, a physics scholar and tenured professor wraps up his work on the latest thesis.

He lovingly turns off the lamp on the teak wood vintage desk. It is cluttered with pieces of crumpled paper and unfinished coffee cups he has collected over the day. He fondly slides his hand over the Tiffany's stained-glass shade. That is his way of remembering his wife every evening; she gifted him the lamp on their 25th wedding anniversary. A devout follower of the Art Nouveau movement, her taste reflected in every household purchase she made.

The last glimpse of light from the setting sun peeks through the long, dark and heavy curtains. With the tall vaulted ceiling, the rich red embroidered fabric adds an air of Victorian lavishness to the professor's office.

Like a child who fears a scolding, he diligently clears the table of everything considered stray or dirt. His wife, who was killed at the mass shooting on campus eight years ago, was like a mother in all aspects of cleanliness. A faint smile lights up his face as he steps down the stairs of the historic department building and into the tree-lined pathway to his apartment.

The cool autumn air refreshes his mind as he ponders his thesis. This one is unique and quite unlike the ones from the past. It does not relate to physics at all. Instead, it chronicles every mass shooting in the world and applies aspects of psychology, mathematics and statistical analysis to derive a correlation between the probability of future mass shootings and prevailing gun laws.

Later in the kitchen, as he stirs pasta sauce made out of fresh tomatoes, he is convinced that his thesis and findings cannot be contested by anyone who bases judgements on scientific facts. He can clearly prove and articulate the primary reasons for the high frequency of mass shootings in the country and the enormity of damage each one causes. The thesis builds on facts related to the number of guns owned in the country, and ease of procuring them - especially automated weapons that can kill hundreds in minutes. The Second Amendment of the Constitution makes the country unique. Interpretations of that precious right are often subject to political and commercial motivations. The alternate belief systems created by these interpretations are the foundational and sole catalysts of the grave situation.

It is impossible, however, to tie gun violence as in mass shootings to gun ownership. The subject of gun ownership begs consideration of a much wider set of historical and cultural truths. Together, the plurality of those truths can contest the conclusions of the thesis by the professor. His research work in the world of physics, a pure form of science, seldom require such social and/or historical considerations.

His guest this evening is a younger lecturer of sociology. Both are looking forward to some carefully chosen Chianti and home-cooked spicy sausage and pasta dinner. And of course, a lively discussion as they always engage in. The professor has a specific motive this evening. Before he prepares his thesis for publication, he wants to hear her perspectives.

Ownership of guns in the country has roots in the culture of famous duels when the Constitution was being formulated, such as the one between Hamilton and Burr. Muzzle loaders and rifle muskets took center stage in the Civil War fought between the Union and Confederate forces. Gun wielding heroes of the world of cowboys followed soon in the Wild West, epitomized, and glorified forever by Clint Eastwood.

Just as a child grows up attached to his security blanket, the nation has grown up with guns by its side. The fear of "they will take away my guns" is historical and sociological, explains the young lecturer as she raises the glass of wine.

She genuinely appreciates the unique but familiar fruity-spicy blend developed in barrels stored in stone bunkers under old buildings in one of the famous alleyways of Siena. She fondly remembers her grandfather who lived his entire life in the famous walled city in Tuscany. Everyone in Italy, like her grandfather, would accept the professor's thesis without a blink in their eyes. But not in the United States, she contests. The plurality of truths matter. Across the modest dinner table, she patiently explains each such truth.

The common theme across the truths is fear of the outside and the need for security with gun ownership. Globalism brings the outside into one's neighborhood, one's own home. The Second Amendment, therefore, must be protected to its fullest and widest extent.

The disdain for gun violence and mass shootings is genuine

but it gets eclipsed by the overarching fear of the outside, the unknown, the push toward globalism. As a result, many conspiracies get rooted firmly in people's minds.

Did man ever land on the moon? May be not and it was just a way to keep NASA funded and the nuclear arms race alive. There were hidden enemies outside that the government wanted to distract the public from.

The nation made history by electing a black president. His ancestral proximity to a foreign country and non-Christian religion led to beliefs in being governed and controlled by someone from the outside.

Fake incidents seem to promote wars abroad. Weapons of Mass Destruction in Iraq was a hoax that was eventually exposed. On the same vein, the 9/11 attacks in New York City could very well be an inside job. These events draw troops and mindshare away from the homeland, exacerbating the need for each citizen to bear arms and protect themselves.

Over a delicious bread pudding dessert that the young professor takes credit for, both the academics agree that a set of disparate facts that reinforce a common sentiment can impact perceptions of truth. As the evening progresses, the physics professor continues to insist on the indelible nature of pure science. The sociology lecturer, on the other hand, maintains her position about the pluralistic nature of truths and how a multitude of globalist initiatives drive people to converge on one summed up truth – that no one should be allowed to take away their guns at any cost.

Later, the professor thanks the sociology expert for her views and bids her goodbye, a somewhat troubled ending to the evening. He returns and settles back on the comfortable armchair. As he ponders if he should publish his thesis, his hand inadvertently turns on the TV. His mind and thoughts drift with the show that is running on his favorite public broadcasting channel. It is about the fascist movement in Europe and the role of propaganda in influencing the truths and rise of the dictators. Fear can lead the nation to the past, even to Nazi-style nationalism. He foresees a troubled future where pure science will become less relevant. And his thesis will be completely overlooked.

Meanwhile, in the apartment on Cornelia Street in West Village, the businessman prepares to exploit the confusions that pluralism brings, shoving pure scientific findings or mathematical formula driven singular facts to the ploy of the elites.

To him, for example, the direct relationship of energy to mass and the speed of light in Einstein's famous formula is a singular fact of no consequence. The dangers of atomic energy to the world – a deduction of the same formula – is however very relevant. It can be spun using multiple approaches including, if needed, coloring the destructions of

Hiroshima and Nagasaki as fake news created to tout the power of one nation and justify global power and governance. The pluralistic nature of truth can be deployed to cast one of the greatest tragedies of modern history as another malicious creation of the elites.

MECHANICAL AND
BODY TRUTHS

The vast majority of the society has been dominated by mechanical truths. Many cross-sections of people, both in the mainstream and the fringes, are being influenced by body truths; they are evolving and multiplying rapidly.

Mechanical truths are immediately visible - they impact lives right here and right now. They are indisputable as a result of their absolute and brazen impact. They are also rigid, cast permanently like in Moses' Tablets of Stone, as inscribed commandments from God. They stand on age-old beliefs.

Body truths, on the other hand, require finer and more

sophisticated perception skills. Often, they are based on deep subjects or models derived from multiple disciplines. Sometimes, they are influenced by individual moods and feelings of the moment. At other times, they are derived from modern data science and sophisticated algorithms that predict future events accurately. To ease understanding by the layman, they may be presented with some levels of abstraction.

There are many steadfast believers to whom mechanical truths are all that matter. Like the ardent and brisk strollers that show up every evening at 5:30 PM on the Chattahoochee River Walk in Columbus, Georgia. They live by the doctrine preached every Sunday at the two hundred churches in the neighborhood.

Their views on what is right versus wrong are unyielding. They do not see disturbing news or ignore them as mere sensationalism. A new breaking news flashes on the electronic billboard perched high on the modern Convention and Trade Center building. It is about priests at a well-known archdiocese and their sentencing for molesting young boys. A middle-aged father with too many wrinkles on his heavy forehead sits on a bench. He is perched sideways to let his aching back stretch; his eyes look blankly at the clouds across the Chattahoochee River. A factory job obsoleted by new technology and then a son lured by the hallucinations of opioid, both gone forever. The flashing banner is unable to catch his attention; it is of no consequence.

The unfathomable sadness and frustration – like those of this father - sink deep into the hearts of these believers in mechanical truths. They carry smart phones in their pockets, received proudly as Mother's or Father's Day gifts or as a perk from work. But they seldom use them to explore the outside world. The phones are meant for receiving urgent calls and, in some cases, urgent communication using text messages about events in the neighborhood. They do not watch the conglomerate-owned television news channels or listen to radio shows affiliated to the right or left wings. They only accept what they can see and touch. The rigor they follow in accepting truths is precision-driven like a mechanical robot.

Auburn University in Alabama is just a 45 minutes-drive from the River Walk. The teachers and students revere the beauty of the Chattahoochee River. They admire the amenities built along the banks lined with trees that burst into bright colors every spring and fall. Their discussions meander like the river itself and they are based on scrupulous historical facts and the vibrant present.

The Chattahoochee has been a food source, a transportation route, a means of spiritual connection for different cultures of people for centuries - the creators of the ancient Kilomoki ruins, to the spiritual Creek Indian encampments, and eventually to be eclipsed by the white settlers who conquered them. Recently, the Chattahoochee has been at the center of a tristate dispute over water usage rights between Florida,

Alabama, and Georgia. The Flint River that connects to the Chattahoochee upstream has already been part of significant controversy as a result of lead poisoning, exacerbated further by tints of racism, corruption, and political bias. Could the Chattahoochee be mired by such controversy as well?

The teachers and students are on the same River Walk as the believers of mechanical truths. But they think differently and dwell on newly derived truths.

Their active and precisely tapping fingers drive their smart phones to expose views on current events by renowned experts. Discussions and views abound in myriads of ways, truths emerging in free form, steered by the curious mind of each participating individual. Riding high on intellectualism and residing on online forums, such passionate revelations and beliefs spread far and wide as body truths.

Mechanical and body truths may converge or go their separate ways.

In one world they converge, causing immense upheaval. They are peddled as synonymous to a sensible path of progress in the future while keeping the nostalgia and legacies of an outdated world firmly intact.

Where the two truths go their separate ways, there is order and peace. Each set of believers live within their bounds and are tolerant of diversity. There is recognition that everyone need not believe in the same truths just as everyone should not be a carpenter - there is a place and significant purpose for farmers too.

It is another very late evening in the West Village. With his favorite TV news channel blasting in the background, the businessman attempts to understand a report about mechanical and body truths to no avail. He just does not have the patience to gauge the differences and their implications. But he knows that he thrives on mayhem and on the basis of just that, places his bet on the world where the two truths converge. As a result, his campaign staffers design their policies based on the glories of the past and ideologies that are grounded on mechanical truths. They then apply methods to defend the same policies utilizing traditional and social media; these are modern tools squarely in the domain of body truths. His political strategy intersects both kinds of truths and causes many disruptions, all in his favor.

TRUTHS TO INFLUENCE BEHAVIOR

The summer of 2015 has been unusually warm in Helsinki. The locals love it but for the software engineer from San Francisco, the thirty-degree centigrade heat is a tad unbearable. After a light breakfast that included the freshest salmon straight from the Baltic, he is contemplating heading to Toolonlahti, a great location for jogging all year round.

Since his college days, he has been obsessed with fitness, eating healthy, and keeping a strict schedule intermingled equally between gym routines and long stretches programming and hacking secure computer networks.

The previous evening, when the Finnair Airbus A321 descended smoothly to land at Helsinki-Vantaa, rainwater flashed across the window in multiple parallel unsteady streams obstructing the view of the lush green forests around Toolonlahti. It was a pleasant evening when he checked into the designer Klaus K Hotel on Bulevardi. While most of Helsinki went quiet on this Sunday evening, this western part of the Kamppi neighborhood was still vibrant well after 11 pm when the engineer had checked into his room with a king bed and two large windows overlooking the shops and cobblestone streets of the Bulevardi.

Toolonlahti is also the place the engineer will meet with the CEO of a big data analytics firm. His last four years of work experience at the giant social media company in the San Francisco Bay Area made him an attractive candidate for a unique job offer.

So far, his talent has been useful in creating applications that help people connect using a social network and enjoy novel ways of sharing their experiences. This new opportunity however could shape the future of the world. That is how the CEO framed the scope of the role and this was thrilling to the engineer.

The meeting is at 11AM. He steps out for a five-mile jog prior to the meeting; the exercise should get his jet-lagged body and mind back to being fresh and alert. Later, after a shower at the hotel, he hops into a bus for the twenty-minute ride to the Toolo bay. Café Kahvila Tyyni, where he will meet the CEO, being one of the most popular cafes' in the bay, shows up immediately on his phone. He taps the screen and saves the location.

When he reaches the café, the CEO, who was waiting, greets him with a wide smile. The distinctly angular jaws on both sides of the grin holds the long face up handsomely. Above the chiseled nose, light wrinkles show a bit of stress on his tanned forehead. His brown hair with stylish streaks of white is brushed back precisely, right above the topmost and longest wrinkle. The white shirt under the dark blue jacket reflects the bright late morning sun, just like the pristine waters of the bay. With eyes focused on and admiring the engineer's muscled physique, he immediately starts a conversation.

The CEO shakes a glass of water he has in his hand and loudly boasts about the freshest tap water in the world. The engineer, wiping sweat persisting from the jog with a towel, acknowledges the proud Finn, fills a glass with sparkling Finnish tap water in solidarity and joins the conversation. The engineer is used to meetings in café's, but this was the first one he started with tap water instead of the typical cappuccino.

The conversation turns serious as the CEO laments the myopic strategy of the giant social media company the engineer works for. The mission to connect people and make their lives better is a façade, he contends, as his white burly eyebrows draw together menacingly on his forehead.

The underlying intent to collect data about its users and then sell them to advertisers and marketers for profit is cheap and unworthy of the power the company wields on society, continues the CEO. The young engineer is intrigued, nods in agreement as he leans forward with interest and respect. The firm the CEO leads has devised a way to use such individual data to actually improve their lives. The challenge he faces is that he does not have access to the needed data. The engineer senses deep frustration and anger as the CEO describes in excruciating details the repeated attempts that he has made to meet executives at the social media company.

Like the sun bursting out suddenly from deep behind the darkest and thickest clouds, a wide grin abruptly and suddenly appears on his face. He boasts this time about a path he has found to break the log jam. And he needs the help the engineer can provide. With a firm grip, the CEO holds the engineer's hand and suggests they step to the counter and get their cups of favorite coffee and continue the conversation in the shaded pathways of the Winter Garden in the north end of the bay.

A short walk around the bay takes the two technocrats into another pride of the Finnish people. The garden features a 19th-century greenhouse, exotic palms, cacti, flowers, and a very unique carp pond. The CEO affirms he has found a way to get access to data that belongs to millions of users. Questions of ethics and privacy begin to swirl in the engineer's mind.

The engineer understands the CEO's motive to benefit individuals that use social media platforms. He acknowledges that selling of individual behavioral data as commodity should be a crime. However, the path to achieving the novel goal the CEO has laid out seems fraught with the same privacy issues. For a change, he takes his turn to speak and expresses his concerns.

The CEO seems to appreciate the assertiveness in the young engineer as he nods in agreement. In response, he reiterates that no one is stopping the misuse currently rampant, including the engineer himself who is contributing to that misuse indirectly. He then emphasizes that the greater good of the society is what will really matter in the end. The morality of those that misuse the data for profit and the callousness of those that give it away under the guise of sophisticated technology will be easily overlooked.

At the end of the trail, as if planned in advance, the CEO summarizes and ends the conversation, shakes the engineer's hands, says the decision is now his, bids goodbye and rapidly walks away into the lush dark green of the woods.

Two months later, as the winter begins to slowly creep in, the software engineer looks at the falling snow. His desk at the analytics firm in Helsinki is right next to the CEO's.

The mission to give benefits and power back to the

individuals in the online society is overwhelming. So, he left sunny California to be in the Nordic city.

Both he and the CEO share the same vision and a long window in the office. They get along well. Unlike the quiet and gently falling snow outside the window, the ideas in both their heads run like torrents. The discussions in the conference rooms may be loud and argumentative, but they are always productive.

The taps on the screens of smart phones, the mouse clicks on the laptop, the likes and comments about the most intimate experiences– all such data collected per individual and then collated and processed collectively using machine learning algorithms can work miracles. The collective beliefs and resulting behavior of groups of people can be influenced and changed. The jihadist group ISIL has already achieved success - utilizing this capability to advance their mission for an Islamic Caliphate. The same recipe can be applied for the good of the society, the CEO confirms with an emphatic tone.

On social media, a few individual loud bullies can silence the voice of the masses who detest any form of violence. A sad consequence, the CEO continues, is that gun violence is a repetitive occurrence in the United States. The effect of social media platforms can be reversed to silence the bullies instead. It will thrive at a crowd-level, and with collective participation. By defeating the loudest bullies, widespread gun reform support can be converted to much needed and useful laws and policies.

At the end of each day, as they leave their offices, the CEO and the engineer feel immensely proud of their mission and work. They become increasingly confident privacy concerns will be addressed, opening up the gates to data from millions of individuals. This is precious data they need to execute their vision. After all, the power of the greater good of the world has to prevail.

It is an unusually warm mid-April day in New York City. The hum of the air conditioner floats above the intense discussion unfolding in the West Village apartment. The businessman sits at the end of the dining table, his face hidden behind both his palms.

The political strategist and other leaders are seated around the table strewn with leftover fast food and bottles of beer and coke. They emphasize to the presidential candidate how they have been successfully pinning the elites and their truths and beliefs to the old world. The new world built on social media is becoming increasingly important and that is what matters. Here, the campaign's home base and target, new truths and alternate beliefs are being propagated much more easily.

The businessman is not convinced. The impact and reach of this new world need to be propelled to a spectacular level to ensure a win at the upcoming presidential election. And time is running out.

The political strategist pulls out an old report by his favorite reporter at the right-wing newspaper he used to head as executive editor. Pointing to the pages bound neatly in a folder, he suggests the use of tactics by jihadist groups like ISIL. The analytics firm in Helsinki becomes the center of attention across the table. If the noble vision of the Finnish CEO can be influenced, his technology can be applied by the campaign staff. The businessman removes his palms from his face, orange, and pale with stress. His eyes however light up at the mention of the CEO. He abruptly stands up, emphasizing how he always likes and gets along with CEOs. He wants to know more about the one in Helsinki.

The political strategist points out that the firm is hurting, being starved of access to valuable data to carry out its mission. The businessman speaks with confidence assuring that he will be able to get the data for the CEO. This will be the data of all individuals from the new world that resides on social media platforms. In return, the firm will have to rapidly grow that world - the target electorate, and his chances of winning. Influenced by new and, if needed, manufactured truths.

Sharp at nine, on another cold morning in Helsinki, the CEO receives a call from the West Village apartment. He takes it in his private conference room. As he listens to the proposal from the political strategist, the CEO's wide forehead creases up with alarming concern.

The CEO is promised access to all the individual data he needs to complete his vision. However, he needs to extend the charter of his firm to political maneuvering.

It is possible to apply the algorithms in this software to manufacture, spread and popularize false ideas. He looks at the engineer through the glass wall in the conference room, deep in thought, probably contemplating another splendid idea to make a software program execute faster. In the bright morning sunlight that trickles through the tall pine trees by the windows, his handsome face loses color.

THE TRUTHS OF
THE GULLIBLES

They have been Taxi drivers for three generations. Now, with differing viewpoints and believing different truths, and they are growing further apart. The youngest in the line almost to a point of no return. He feeds on the gullible, influencing their truths.

The only son to his Sikh parents, he has recently transitioned to be a Ride App driver, much to the subdued discern of his father, and vehement abhorrence of his grandfather. The older two generations cannot understand the floating state of the youngest – he is neither an employee of a company, nor does he have his own company. Yet, he sustains a living, much busier picking up and dropping passengers - more of them per day than any of his two immediate ancestors.

The grandfather knew every nook and corner of Nariman Point and Colaba in Mumbai; the two well-known metropolises at the affluent end of the long stretch of a seaside road. It is called the Queen's necklace. At night the lights from numerous buildings and shops along this stretch of the road glitter like the diamonds in the necklace of the Queen that had ruled this British colony for many years. He had a photographic memory of small streets, intersections, unique shops, homes, and their owners. The passenger just had to mention a few pointers before the destination could be located. He knew the names of many owners of street corner shops – they were always there to guide him if he lost his way on rare occasions.

The father, on the other hand, drove a taxi in the more structured neighborhoods of Pittsburgh, Pennsylvania and did well without having to exploit his memory to the degree his father had to. Lately, he has learned to use GPS and maps on his phone to locate addresses of passengers more easily.

The distress over the recent action of the Ride App driver is also related to his choice of the profession itself, and his unwillingness to break away from the not-so-profitable business of driving passengers. A bright student, he was admitted to the engineering school at Carnegie Mellon. He dropped out suddenly in his senior year after consistently being an honors student.

Like his grandfather, his mind always wants to get to know nooks and corners in great detail. In his case, however, it is the far reaches of the Internet, the secrets and conspiracies that live there, uncovering and comprehending each episode. After all, he has to find meaning in the confused state of the world. Driving passengers is just a means to that end.

His sense of dress can at best be described as sloppy. His shoelaces often come undone; his socks are stretched unevenly. Always a jeans and t-shirt guy, he also wears a long sideburn on his otherwise clean-shaven and remarkably pale face. His features are sharp, his diction is laden with rich vocabulary, and if his hair wasn't black, as he says, he could have passed off as a Caucasian. He has been a Ride App driver for nine months now and his rating is 4.98. The passengers that ride with him always marvel at the depth of his knowledge about world affairs. The conversations go deep and become very involved; passengers reach their destinations without a dull moment.

Lately, riding on his increased confidence and ability to capture the passenger's attention – as if hypnotizing them - he has ventured into experimenting with their minds and beliefs.

The Delta Airlines flight from Tokyo's Haneda Airport to Pittsburgh International Airport is close to fifteen hours long. It is a summer late afternoon in Pittsburgh – cooled off substantially by a bout of thunder and rain. The Ride App driver is specifically looking for a passenger who is familiar with Japan; his conversation would start with intriguing facts about the land of the rising sun. He receives a ride request on the Ride App. He earnestly hopes the passenger is from the Delta flight that has just landed.

About fifteen minutes after, a perky financial analyst hops into the back seat of his car. He enters the destination on his smartphone: it is in the village of Sewickley he has never been to. With the work commuters beginning to fill the highway in swarms, traffic is heavy. It will be a thirty-minute ride, or less. Just enough to experiment with her mind. They greet each other and immediately begin a conversation.

The car glides out of the airport and into the highway, bare-ly making a sound. The brand-new Ford Focus, purchased on a loan from the Ride App Company, is a hybrid. She first breaks the silence, praising the modern interior design of the car and the smooth ride on freshly made repairs and a thick layering of tar on Highway 376.

The long flight has not eroded a bit of the excitement from the very successful meetings she had with clients in Japan. She thoroughly enjoyed presenting and negotiating with the gently nodding, scrupulous Japanese clients in sparkling clean offices with glass walls. She was perched up high in the formidable, tall buildings of well-known multinational companies, in the crowded and bustling cities of Osaka and Shinagawa. Later, she mingled with professionals in numer-ous meetings at a conference by the beaches and sands of picturesque Okinawa.

She observes the driver's long well-groomed fashionable sideburns, and the very feminine pink colored T-shirt. Her shapely figure under the flowery and lace bordered white and blue dress catches his attention as she further stretches and leans backward lazily. From the corner of his eye, he notices a silver necklace descending over smooth skin and sweat to an inviting cleavage. He resets his brain and focuses his eyes on the road and conversation ahead. All he needs is thirty minutes to experiment his ideas on her, so he hopes there will be traffic as the evening approaches. Can her beliefs be questioned easily, and can they be influenced? In other words, is she gullible?

She is further intrigued by him when she learns that he had lived in rural Japan for almost a year, taking time off from college. When in Sendai, the capital of Miyagi, it was incredibly easy for a young foreigner like him to mingle because most of the local population are in their twenties, untethered from age old culture. The mention of Sushi as her favorite food prompts him to boast how Japanese delicacies notably hiyashi chuka and gyutan originated in Miyagi. While she knows financial analysis to the last detail, her knowledge of Japanese cuisine is limited to Sushi and Sapporo only. With the confidence of a person who knows Japan like a local, when he retorts that Sushi was actually first concocted in Tibet and Sapporo was first brewed in Germany, she almost believes him. He chuckles abruptly, saying he was joking. She is somewhat shaken both by the loudness of his laughter and her own naïveté.

Jokes aside, there are many things governments lead us to believe that are not true, he continues.

The invasion of Iraq was not about Saddam Hussein. It was about oil and the uprising he was leading that would peg world economies on the price of oil instead of the US Dollar. That would make the United States financially less relevant. Saddam had to be taken out, at any cost.

The government also needed a way to redeem themselves from the NASA fiasco and move on. That catches her attention again, he notices on the rear-view mirror. What do you mean NASA fiasco? After all it is a well-respected organization, a jewel that the world looks up to. NASA spent so many billions of dollars of taxpayer money - he corrects her - that after the debacle of the space program they had to mockup Apollo 11 and the walk on the moon by Niel Armstrong. When she asks for proof, he points to many You Tube videos and other links on the Internet, working his fingers dangerously on the phone as the car maneuvers through narrow winding roads leading to the rural destination.

She is somewhat relieved as they enter beautiful Sewickley. The village is a throwback to yesteryear with its picturesque Main Street, locally owned shops, and a sprawling community park. It is a charming place that, in some ways, has been frozen in time. Lush green trees line the wide sidewalks. She likes to live in the yesteryear. This is where she grew up. She tends to believe in what she is told. She assumes the truth in what she reads and notices, and honesty in people she comes across. She loves the community and is pained to see that lately, it is suffering. Lost jobs and drugs are driving people out of the township. For her young age, she is uniquely a woman of the older, traditional world.

The thirty-five minutes with the Ride App driver pass quickly. Each of his narratives about happenings around the world is astoundingly revealing to her. When she finally disembarks from the car parked by the sidewalk on Amicitia Lane, she is somewhat relieved. She cannot deny that he is rather intelligent with deep knowledge in many areas, and he is friendly. On the Ride App, she gives him 4 stars and 15% tip.

As the driver makes a couple of successive right turns to exit the village, he declares his mission a success. The conspiracies and lies he threw at her gently unnerved her as expected. They affected her own beliefs and she started questioning if everything she knew all along was true. She has been invited to participate in the new world and she will no doubt explore the validity of his narratives in online and social media platforms.

The grandfather is firmly grounded in the old world. The grandson Ride App driver's life and opinions are rooted in the new world; he is a soldier and proponent of evolving truths; he is a missionary fixated on growing the world he lives in. The father is stuck in the nebulous middle world. Both he and the financial analyst from Sewickley are confused and susceptible. The truths of the old world and the new are at odds. They must cling to some to make sense of the world they live in. They become gullible.

In the apartment in West Village, the campaign team is unanimous in their appreciation that youngsters like the Ride App driver can be effectively utilized in the businessman's quest to be president. Credulous people like the older father and the young financial analyst are clear targets for the campaign - their votes in the upcoming election are convertible and vital.

THE TRUTH BEHIND
FREE THINGS

Bob Seger's "Down on Main Street" plays in the juke-box at the end of a long corridor. The rustic pine log floors and walls still smell fresh in the seventy-eight-year old bar called Spyglass Tavern. It stands on Main Street in Prineville, Oregon, across from a timber mill that ceased operation in the late nineties.

A blonde goatee elongates the thin face of a young logger turned bike-shop owner, a native of Prineville. In one of the bar tables, he sits shoulder-to-shoulder with a visiting filmmaker in his late fifties. Unlike the bohemian-style long beard on the lean-chiseled face of the logger, the film-maker's French version is thick and well-cropped; it hides the chubbiest portions of his face. Thick black rectangular rimmed glasses round up his distinctive look as an artist.

The bike-shop owner is remarkably informed about the turbulent history of the town. Livelihood came from selling products conceived and produced using hard working hands, shoulders, and legs. He is intrigued by the recent transformations; so is the filmmaker. The economy now centers around new and incredibly rich corporate giants that do not sell any products.

Over locally crafted beer, they discuss their next project – a film about how this tiny town went from logging and livestock to bits and bytes, a timber town transformed by two massive billion-dollar companies into a recreational hub of mountain bikers and craft brewers.

Prineville, named for an early settler, was built on timber; its proximity to the railroad and abundance of pine trees propelled it to a town of enormous opportunity. Timber fellers and ranchers flocked into Prineville, as did rockhounds collecting agates in the volcanic high country. Like many milling and mining towns in the mid-west and the Rust Belt, Prineville was eventually destined to become a ghost town. Until just a few years ago, it was poised to become yet another victim of technology, globalization, and regulation.

Then, a large social media company from California came along, attracted as a fly-bait to a trout, by the significantly lower cost of power and cooling in the Prineville region.

The company provides software-based services and makes money off user behavioral data, crunching them in huge data centers for valuable market intelligence. And those football field-sized data centers can consume enough energy to power a small town of ten thousand people.

One of those data centers is perched on the edge of a bluff above where the Crooked River curls into a canyon. Above, the Ochoco Mountains loom where the sun rises heralding the long days of summer. The social media company's sleek buildings are decorated with politically correct and socially just messages and monster sized murals, with the company's mantra and mission interleaved. The idea is to project they are one and the same.

A fleet of bicycles are parked out front, standing in perfect lines. Past them is a shoal of pool tables laid out lavishly across a sea-blue colored, sprawling break room. The ambience is casual, reflective of a relaxed culture, indicative of a "social company".

The hum of the machines and a blast of cold air escape into the quiet and cozy break room every time one of the large metal doors open and close. The massive halls behind the doors have rows and rows of machines. Each machine is a rectangular shaped metallic box and carry sophisticated electronics that generate heat. A series of small fans mounted on one wall of the box pumps cool air over the heated components. Each of them is a server or a storage unit. There are hundreds of thousands of them stacked up in racks. Living up to their names, they process each request from the social media platform users and store each typed letter or uploaded picture as the users post their status to their families and friends.

Between each row are long corridors, some facing the blinking lights in the decorative front face of the machines and racks, while others are designed to provide access to cables, power switches, pull-on trays and screens that display the health of the server and storage units. Humans, and increasingly more robots, walk the corridors constantly, ensuring each post from the anxious user is quickly recorded, stored and made available to their intended targets.

The targets are, however, not always friends and family members. The targets are also software and systems that utilize artificial intelligence to capture behavioral trends useful to marketers of products who can then deliver more targeted advertisements. The product – that generates many billions of dollars each quarter of a financial year – is in fact an amalgamation of behaviors of individual users. It is an abstract and invisible product not visible to the common masses. But it is incredibly valuable in the new world.

The raw earth, the forests of pine trees, the rivers and the mountains, the flies and the trout, the fishermen and the loggers, the locals and visitors sipping ice-cold beer in Spyglass Tavern are subjects of the old world. Their reach is limited to the neighborhoods of Prineville. The constantly humming machines in the air-conditioned halls of the sleek buildings create bubbles of millions of instances of the virtual and online world, the all-powerful new world that reaches every corner of the modern society.

Under a dim lantern-shaped lamp, the bike-shop owner pulls out his laptop from a worn-out leather bag. Switching back and forth between the old and new worlds has become a norm for him, he explains to the filmmaker. In the old world, people like the filmmaker are real people to rub shoulders with and share real-world experiences like the crispy bitterness of locally brewed crafts. His customers from the new world are casual and professional mountain bikers that hail from distant cities like Munich, Copenhagen, and Colombo as much as they do from neighboring Bend and Seattle. His social media pages are rich with information and recommendations about local biking trails and adventures. The casual and recreational bikers often indulge in boasting achievements. The numerous likes and accolades from friends make them instant celebrity cyclists as their photo-shopped pictures increasingly project the flair of Lance Armstrong. This causes a fame-envy spiral as more users venture into the sport, attempting more glamorous posts. The exposure out of this swirling phenomenon is immense as bikers who post or like experiences on his pages bring their entire group of friends and relatives as future target customers.

Not all that visit his website can be targets as prospective customers. The social media platform and its intelligent algorithms running in the humming machines know specific behaviors of each friend and relative and lists those that are most likely to come biking to the pristine mountains of Prineville. He pays the social media company a monthly fee of a few hundred dollars for such valuable market analytics data, contributing to the multibillions of dollars of revenue the company commands.

Without paying a dime, the citizens of the new world, the users of social media, lavishly and recklessly use up the resources in the billion-dollar facilities of Prineville. There isn't a product to be purchased, but the resources available at their disposal - to post their feelings and experiences, to live in the new world - are infinite.

The intrigued filmmaker has a sudden moment of revelation. The characters and behaviors of new world individuals can be transcribed into digital bits that the servers and storage units in large data centers can crunch on. These bits are the products of the social media company. They are sold to business owners like the goateed gentleman next to him, still immersed deep in the world inside his laptop. If the behavior of the users could be influenced to take up recreational biking in unique regions like Prineville, the bike-shop owner's dreams to franchise and expand into larger cities like Portland and Washington can be fulfilled significantly faster.

The revelation continues in the cozy dim lights of Spyglass Tavern. The social media company takes the monthly fee from the bike-shop owner as a token and the behavioral data related to his clients as the real meat — what drives the valuation of the company and makes many shareholders millionaires.

The filmmaker concludes that the true philosophy and mission of the social media company is: "If I can influence your behavior, I will give you the world for free". The walls of the sleek data center buildings in Prineville are decorated floor to ceiling with murals of abstract figures that look half alien and half comical. The true philosophy and mission are invisible.

In the lobby of the data center building, the filmmaker feels like an ant as he stands under one such mural towering above him and the receptionist. The giant wall is filled up by a massive figure of a young girl with an alien head, sitting on a bicycle with square wheels. Fine abstract art, he thinks, to belittle and confuse you.

Originally from Berlin, he is steeped in the history of fascism in Europe. He sees a stark resemblance to the worlds of Hitler and Mussolini. The two European dictators influenced the behavior of the masses to favor their own interests. The fascist leaders used a constant barrage of propaganda and falsehoods. Then, the medium for influencing opinions was the radio and the news media in each family's living room. Now, it is smart phones and the social media on each individual's finger tips. The medium has changed but the intent is the same.

During the period of fascism in Europe, the radio and news companies barely made a dime; it was all in for the dictators. In the new paradigm, the social media companies capitalize eyeballs and finger taps to propel themselves to never before seen levels of success. Vociferous leaders, especially the controversial ones who spread propaganda using the software platform, only help their cause.

The filmmaker shakes the bike-shop owner out of the online world, back to reality. He asks if the social media platform could be used to influence voting behaviors of the people who live in the new world, just like the fascists did ninety years ago. The bike-shop owner returns a blank stare – the incessant quest to grow his business make the potentially dark underlying philosophy and mission of the social media company invisible to him.

Three thousand miles east, at the apartment in West Village, an intense dialogue emerges from far corners of the living room, like a gathering storm.

The catch phrase is - drain the swamp. Especially in Washington DC. The elitist interests in oil and Exxon, in pharmaceuticals and Merck, in corporate finance and Goldman Sachs must all be wiped out. The businessman concludes that the need for financial support from these powerful groups can be supplanted by a new class of companies.

These modern mega companies can not only get him elected to office, but also sustain him as the president during his tenure.

For example, he can effectively utilize their software platforms to influence opinions and behaviors and keep his base firmly behind him. He will do so by constantly manufacturing new truths that only favor him. Most importantly, these companies will eventually boost his net worth. Just like his hit reality show on television. But on a far greater scale.

This new class comprises social media companies with hundreds of millions of users, and one of them with more than two billion. While draining the swamp, their interests must be protected at all costs.

TRUTHS DEFINED
BY PLAY RULES

The running back plays offence. He advances aggressively down the field and at the right instant receives the oval-shaped ball by hand, thrown with amazing precision by the quarter back. This is the crux of excitement in American Football. In European Football, the same applies except that the ball is round and passing is conducted by the feet of the midfield and center forward players. The same feet are also used to run and advance, making play more complicated and less predictable. An audience watching the two sports needs to get used to entirely different sets of rules. For example, in one, the use of hands is legal while in the other it is a foul and causes an outright penalty if used close enough to the goal posts. Fans who love and watch both sports need to be in two alternate states of mind.

Imagine two large stadiums each filled with a hundred thousand fans. One is Michigan Stadium in Ann Arbor – an undisputed favorite for American Football. The other is Camp Nou located in Barcelona, Spain, the home of many European Soccer tournaments. Inside the stadiums, the enthusiasts live in a world where the star players are gods. All emotions and gestures are purely geared toward winning a game in about a couple of hours. The audience in each realm are in a bubble of excitement and short-term gratification, with completely contrarian views of what is right from wrong on the field.

Outside the stadiums, the world is much broader. Not only by the sheer number of billions of people but also the collective state of mind. The subjects of passion and ache span a much wider spectrum and each emotion stretches over the lifetime of an individual. Most of them go to work for a livelihood, others prepare for the next class or exam in the quest to gain knowledge. Many others go out on hikes to enjoy nature, while some recuperate from their injuries of the body or the mind. And some others just do nothing and stare at the cotton white clouds in a pristine blue sky or piercingly bright stars floating in menacingly dark space.

The hundred thousand individuals in the galleries and the players, coaches, officials, and referees in the field inside Michigan Stadium form a new world that lasts the duration of the game. Another similar new world exists simultaneously in Camp Nou. And the billions outside those two new worlds constitute the genesis – the old and traditional world. Everyone inside the two stadiums are tethered to the old world, but for the hours they are in the game, the bind is blissfully lost. Inside each new world, the individuals supporting opposing teams can become enemies in an instant just because they passionately support and desire two contrasting outcomes.

The middle-aged bookstore owner is a native of Ann Arbor. Her downtown Main Street shop is unique in that it also features a cozy tearoom. Her mother, an Englishwoman, inculcated the belief that good fiction and flavorful Darjeeling tea went hand in hand. An old Smith Corona typewriter sits on a small square oak table in a secluded corner, inviting patrons to compose their thought-of-the-day in an old-fashioned way.

Another favorite in the bookstore is shelf number six – it has a collection of books about the history and rise of the Michigan Wolverines. She is a diehard fan and will not miss a game, rain or shine. On the aisle of that shelf, she is usually on the hunt for visiting Wolverine fans. On this day, she is lucky and finds one. Both of them marvel at the strength and skills of defensive tackle Chris Wormley. With a six feet five inch and more than three-hundred-pound frame, he is astounding in all three fronts – dexterity, agility, and technique. She convinces the retired construction worker from

Detroit to go to the 11 AM game next morning, this time against the Wisconsin Badgers.

As they drive together through late morning fog to the Michigan Stadium in a comfortable Cadillac, they also discuss their past. He is an auto mechanic-turned-construction worker, thanks to the downturn of the nineties in the auto industry. She has been a liberal all her life and an active supporter of cannabis laws, specifically the use of marijuana for medical purposes.

As they walk into the stadium through gate G5, the noise level inside is deafening, drowning their conversation and differences in views. They enter the new world; the electrifying environment untie them unknowingly from the world outside they have been so intimately been part of just a moment ago. The bright morning sun and the cheering of the crowd are all that matter now, as their prowling eyes quickly locate Wormley, their idol.

Salvador Dali's museum in Figueres is both strange and grand. Large white stones shaped like eggs represent life and stand tall on the colorful walls of the building, as if they are statues. The walls guard the museum like a fort and are decorated with figures that represent loaves of bread, stuck haphazardly on the smooth magenta surface like buttons.

For nineteen years, a student of this quaint and small town

has often walked the shadows of these most unnatural walls. He has never paid much attention to the eccentricities in Dali's life and art. He does, however, always notice the consistent kink in the gelled moustache of his political science professor at the University of Barcelona. It is shaped after Dali's in a blatant way. Catalonian style as the two friends would agree proudly.

During the morning break from the curriculum, a dish or two of tapas, cigarettes and double shots of expresso compound their loud arguments. To the disdain of fellow students and professors in the vicinity, it is always about the likely outcome of an upcoming soccer match. Futbol Club Barcelona, commonly referred to as FC Barcelona and colloquially known as Barça, is Spain's most famous soccer team, led by its star forward Lionel Messi. Later that afternoon in Camp Nou, the student and the professor are among the hundred thousand screaming their support for Barca and Messi.

If the bookstore owner and construction worker from Ann Arbor are transported to Camp Nou, each initiative and tactic by the FC Barcelona players will be deemed strange, illegal, worthy of penalties. It will take them a while to adjust to the new rules of the game. In fact, it is impossible to adjust to the new truths for the mere two hours inside the stadium. The same is true if the student and the professor from Barcelona were to be accidentally transported to

Michigan Stadium in the middle of the Wolverines versus Badgers game.

Outside the stadiums however, the rules of living and survival are the same. Patience and tolerance abound as discussions and adjustments can take a lifetime. The four sports fans can be friends for life. In other words, many conflicts arise quickly in the new worlds, not so in the old world where time is stretched, and values are grounded in realities of everyday life.

In the apartment in West Village, the political strategist with unruly straight hair has no specific interest in the talented Football teams or eclectic crowds in the large stadiums. However, the variations in what is perceived as truths, rules, and law matter immensely. The new policies by the presidential candidate will require a new set of truths to stand on. Otherwise, they will appear erratic or even illegal. Like one stadium at a time, an instance of a new world can be created with a new set of truths. New policies can then be quickly released backed up by the new truths as foundations. Only individuals in the old world or another instance of a new world could object and find the new policies strange, odd, or even illegal. But that will not matter just like the opinions of the bookstore owner and construction worker would not in Camp Nou. Or those of the student and the professor from Barcelona in Michigan stadium.

Rules to be played by, and what is perceived and accepted as truths in one world can be vastly different from another. That is the decree to be spread rapidly from the apartment in West Village.

Individuals that live in worlds different from where the businessman choses to live as president will be confused and disappointed daily. Because, the new president will partner with dictators, brand generational allies as enemies, and recruit foreign powers and entities to defeat or disgrace political opponents.

In the new world he will live in and promote, the radically different policies and unconventional means to implement them will always be well accepted. Those individuals that are forced from another world into the newly created world for the businessman will be unable to discern how the rules and truths of this world are constructed and validated. They will complain that the players – the leader and his administration – are not ethical and violate the principles of the office. It will not matter after all – perched on his favorite armchair like a king, the businessman grins with growing confidence.

THE DEATH OF A DAY HOME

Tree-lined Lincoln Avenue in Willow Glen boasts of many unique shops. Among specialty food stores and clothing boutiques is a place called The Macarons. It is a setting sweet and colorful as the French confections, filled with the chatter and screams of children who come there to play, and their parents to apply much needed trims to disorderly young hair.

The two hair salon owners – one from Iran and the other from Ohio - have been together operating The Macarons for more than twelve years. To the regular customers, the two experienced women are expert hair stylists, friendly neighbors and patient babysitters combined. They specialize in keeping their very young subjects distracted as their carefully maneuvering fingers and scissors work diligently to get the job done, one head of hair at a time.

Lincoln crosses Willow Avenue which cuts through a residential neighborhood with tall old Eucalyptus and wide-girthed Willow trees. At the end of the neighborhood, just before where the smaller streets begin to merge on to highway 280, there is a two-acre property. At one end of the property, stand the sprawling and well-maintained residences of the Sisters of the Holy Family. The sisters own the property that includes a school building on the other end and an orchard of lush fruit-bearing lemon and cherry trees in between. A children's day home, funded partially by the sisters, operate in the school building. Over 107 years, the day home has served the families of Willow Glen and adjoining communities.

On a hot and unusually muggy August evening, the day home board members trickle into the empty front lobby of the school building. The board is composed of a desired mix of experienced professionals from the non- and for-profit worlds. The principal, appointed four years ago by the board, has called an emergency meeting. A Hispanic lady in her late forties, she prides in both her silky-smooth skin and perfect English diction. Always very articulate and with a smile that vigorously brightens the shine on her cheeks, she can put anyone at ease in a minute. This evening however, she seems deeply occupied in her office that adjoins the lobby.

The principal does not seem interested in greeting the board members. It is very uncharacteristic of her. She is occupied with a last-minute assignment for a thesis on the history of the Hispanic LGBT community in California. She enrolled into a doctorate program at the San Jose State University fourteen months ago.

The unwelcoming attitude makes the visiting board members somewhat uncomfortable. The mood is somber as they gather around an oval-shaped mahogany table, chipped and scratched in many places over years of use.

The chairman of the board takes the designated chair at the far end of the table. She is a member of the Sisters of the Holy Family, in her early fifties and younger than most of her colleagues. The expensive Burberry glasses sit gracefully on her sharp nose flanked by high cheek bones and the angle of her rather long jaw. Her handsome almost manly face is contoured elegantly by well-groomed cropped white hair.

Pictures on the light beige walls in the conference room showcase the century-old history of the school, leading to the centenary celebrations at the far end, behind where the chairman sits. The room has no windows and the lighting is dim but that does not fail to accentuate the pinnacle the day home reached in its 100th year of operation. Ever since, increased competition from academically oriented schools in the neighborhoods have created new challenges. But the day home has proudly withstood the many trials it has faced over the years, keeping its non-profit and care-first philosophy intact, thanks to the support by wealthy sponsors and die-hard proponents of Willow Glen.

This evening however, the board is about to discuss bankruptcy. The sponsors and proponents are refusing to support the day home any further. Even the Sisters of the Holy Family want a way out, proposing that the property be sold off. With a cup of coffee in her hand, the principal enters the room. Her face bright as usual, featuring the same warm and comforting smile that the board members fell for when they hired her.

Half-way through the meeting, the board members face a conundrum.

In the name of charity that the Sisters promote daily, the Hispanic principal has – over the last four years – aggressively shifted the student population to those that cannot afford to pay tuition. As a result, the day home has increasingly relied on funding from the county and not-for-profit organizations to run and manage its operations. The demographics of the school has changed to more than 80% Hispanic. 70% of the day care attendees do not pay a dime. Yet, the school is expected to somehow maintain the caregivers' and teachers' salaries, and the high expenses related to serving of healthy freshly cooked meals daily in the large well-furnished dining hall.

The situation is quite unlike the earlier demographic where predominantly wealthy white parents from the Willow Glen neighborhood not only paid tuition but contributed hefty sums at fund raiser events. Financially, this is a disaster. From a charity perspective, serving children from poorer families is novel and inspirational. The board members stay silent, being extra cautious not to make a comment that may be construed as racially biased. There is no way out. The day home has to shut its doors for good in two months or less.

Back on Lincoln Avenue, a middle-aged teacher from the day home and her two children enter The Macarons. The Iranian stylist greets her promptly and offers lollipops to the ten-year-old boy and six-year-old girl - two of her most loyal clients. She also notes that the teacher is not her usual pleasant self; she seems annoyed and distressed.

The teacher sits on a leather armchair in the corner by one of the small TV sets that run Bugs Bunny cartoons all day long. That is one way the hairstylists keep their young clients distracted. The teacher is oblivious to the incessant quacking dialogue of Daffy Duck and the ensuing laughter of her children.

Abruptly, she divulges the news to the hair stylists. The 108-year-old children's day home where she has been working the past fourteen years has run out of money and will shut its door at the end of the summer. The middle eastern stylist is surprised. She steps closer to the teacher, places a supporting hand on the shoulder and inquires further. The teacher curtly responds - if it was not for the Mexicans, this jewel of Willow Glen would be just fine like it has been for more than a century. The salon owner is taken aback by a comment that seems racist, but she keeps her calm and continues to console the teacher.

The day home board members are elites, would carefully craft their responses, and be politically correct. They stay quiet and numb in the old, traditional world. The middle-aged schoolteacher, on the other hand, feels the pain, misses the good days at the day home. She logs into her social media account and posts many pictures of the day home over the years and laments its sad demise. Many residents of Willow Glen feel the same way.

The posts on social media about the day home and the pursuits of the Hispanic principal go viral. They catch the attention of the businessman, the political strategist, and his campaign staff as they prepare late night in the West Village apartment for the party's pre-election convention. They make sure an invitation goes out to the middle-aged ex schoolteacher.

THE NEW STORY TELLERS

The fresh-out-of-school UC Berkeley engineer was a 4.0 GPA student. He is also a fitness freak, follows a three hundred sit-ups and a thousand jump-rope regime at each sunrise.

The drive from his modest apartment in Foster City to work requires him to cross the seven-mile stretch of what used to be the longest bridge in the world when it was built and when his grandfather was born. Every morning, over the concrete bridge, he crosses a section of California's San Francisco Bay. In the midsection that also used to be a drawbridge, his abhorrence of the view around peaks.

Every day of the week, he detests the dull, flat view of the still ashen back waters. Disorderly growths of tall brown grass on gloomy gray sands on each end of the bridge only dampen his mood. The snow-white sprinkling of occasionally visiting seagulls tries to break the monotony. But not enough.

This experience is quite in contrast to the spectacular views from most other bridges in the vicinity. Sharp green and red cliff edges contour expansive blue skies that curve down gently into the Pacific, spilling the grandeur of the colors into the white foamy waters that continuously smack dark rocks and sometimes ancient wrecked ships.

Where the bridge and melancholic experience end, on the very edge of the San Francisco Peninsula, is the sprawling campus of the social media company he works for. His parents are proud and often boast about his incredibly high salary and perks to their friends and colleagues. The young engineer, on the other hand, thinks his role at the conglomerate company is nothing more than that of a pawn in a game of chess, or just another cog in a machine with many massive gears that move a conveyor belt carrying world-changing agendas.

At the entrance of the office campus, the ordinary hand-gesture logo, and an inauspicious street name, that glorifies computer hackers, appear on a billboard. The sign appears temporary, by design. The young engineer ponders the street name in the light of how the country is divided like never before, thanks to unethical stealing of personal information by hackers. The street is less than 100 meters long and makes a nervous attempt to glorify hackers.

The name and logo on the company billboard that greet the workers and the visitors appear fungible, almost the work of someone indecisive. It is far from being fixed in solid concrete with deeply etched solid letters one would expect adorning the face of a large company. The genesis of the company, after all, was unethical hacking of University computers by a few intelligent geeks who lacked social skills. Ironically, they have devised a method of how society interacts and behaves today.

A hundred meters past the inconspicuous entry, the world changes dramatically.

The young engineer's bright blue mini cooper glides past the unique five-way intersection into the campus that is bounded by a circular road. Odd numbered office buildings are on the right and even numbered are on the left. The engineer is directed by a traffic personnel as he turns right, headed toward building 17. As he turns, he notices many enthusiastic visitors standing in front of the billboard and taking selfies hurriedly. The pictures will be posted quickly on the social media company's very popular platform – before they are chased away by the traffic control people who seem to guard the campus as if it was Buckingham Palace.

A left turn from the circular road leads him to a parking lot in front of a row of brightly colored buildings with long rows of square windows. The front of Building 17 is painted a modest light gray with the adjacent wall at a ninety-degree joint featuring turquoise blue. There is also yellow and crimson red in the distance, together the effect is meant to replicate the buildings on Nyhavn in Copenhagen.

The engineer drives past many open parking slots reserved for electric cars and expectant mothers. He finally parks facing the west, away from the scorching late August morning sun. It is 8 AM sharp. Tall, dark, and long buses begin to roll in like a line of centipedes, directed by traffic personnel to a designated part of the parking area. Employees who like to avoid driving in the nasty commute-time traffic trickle down from the bus and head toward their respective buildings. Some with backpacks behind them contemplate the cafeteria and the breakfast choices of the day. Others with disheveled hair, open laptops, and unfinished work head straight to their desks.

Tucked away in unknown corners of these colorful buildings at one of the edges of the San Francisco Peninsula are the new gods of the online world.

One of them – titled Vice President or VP of Infrastructure - resides in Building 17 and directs the work of the young engineer and many hundreds of his colleagues. From his perch of absolute power, the VP weaves fairy tales of a new world that resides on the infrastructure of computers and software that his army of engineers are building.

In a way, the VP's motives are similar to Hans Christian

116

Anderson who constructed immortal fairy tales for all ages from his home in Nyhavn 67 and 18. He actually prides himself to be in the likeness of Anderson. A prominent large nose separates droopy eyes under a forehead lengthened by a receding hairline. His ears carry strikingly large earlobes, a sign of being a good listener and therefore wise like the Buddha. The hair above each ear is curled symmetrically and stylishly; the thickness and perfection of the curls mimic a judge's wig from the Victorian ages. The smooth skin of the nostrils give way to deep wrinkles that curve down to the side of his lips blackened by many years of smoking. A few thinner ridges on the brown skin rise from the darker circles under his eyes and run down parallel to the well-formed jawline, completing the marked contour of his face.

Each third-party supplier of computer hardware and software components used to build and run the infrastructure carefully listen to and yield to the words of wisdom that emerge from the powerful mind of the VP. The fairy tales he weaves can be spun effectively only on the very best components from these suppliers. So, he must wield full control over them. And he does, thanks to the enormous power of his platform that is already changing the world, by influencing minds, one opinion at a time. Each tale generates a new opinion and a new truth, spun out efficiently by his infrastructure.

From his desk, the engineer waves at the VP and wishes him good morning. He browses through one more time the new algorithm he fine-tuned last night. He checks in the source code into the company repository. Instantly, it becomes one of the prized intellectual properties of the company. It will fuse in with many other ancillary software features his colleagues have developed. The amalgamation will create a vital metric about the users of the social media platform. The metric will derive behavior patterns and predict how certain opinions can be easily perceived as facts. In other words, how new truths can be created.

The engineer only sees his own work. He does not know how his meticulous work gels with complementary shards of computer logic in python code running across hundreds of thousands of computers in the infrastructure. He is blissfully unaware of how the product of his knowledge and mind becomes part of a plot in the tale being woven. Only the VP and those above him in the organizational hierarchy know how the work of each bright engineer creates a speckle of magic dust in the fairy tale.

A few haphazard streams of westerlies blow all the way from the circular campus in the San Francisco Peninsula to New York City. Spatters of magic dust cross the breadth of the nation – from west to east, from coast to coast, across the heartland, the mid-west, and the rust belt - and settle on the roof of the apartment in West Village.

It is dawn and the businessman has finally fallen asleep. His fingers move slowly and unsurely on the TV remote still on his hand. In his deep sleep, he sees a fairy tale nation where his face and his voice are on every television screen, billboard, on the stages of Broadway theatres, every picture frame in every household, and on all the screens in movie theatres. The elites and their followers flee the nation, across the northern and southern borders, over tall walls, and treacherous forests. Immigration officers erect new barriers to stop them from returning. As a result, streets and neighborhoods become sparkling clean. There is resolute order and glaring consistency everywhere - in the structure and contour of people's faces, the color of their skins, the quality and shape of the clothes they wear, and the accents they use when they talk.

INTERLUDE I:
MIDAS TOUCH - ACQUIRED

The strategy to beat the truths of the elites worked. It is a splendid dream come true that has jolted the established and pulled the rug from under every pundit. The businessman's visions from the West Village apartment persist but now in the southwest corner on the second floor of the Whitehouse, in the President's bedroom.

He is partially awake, confidently aware that he is actually there. His exuberance knows no bounds for he now controls the most powerful platform on the planet. While his staunch supporters await his next move to revert the nation back to past greatness, the President is contemplating another to amass personal wealth at breakneck speed.

He has created a world with a new set of truths. Truths that are most impactful right at the instant it is delivered. It is a world without memory that lives on social media. This platform to grow wealth virally - as a result of wielding unfettered power over tens of millions of followers and trending in media channels constantly - is more powerful than the golden touch of King Midas of Phrygia.

Since he won the election, he has been on the news every second. The effect of his constant presence on TV and social media upends center and left-wing politics and their policies. Branded as conspiracies meant to elevate only the interest of the elites, the work of the previous administration begins to be dismantled at a feverish pace.

The new President has caused one of the greatest election upsets in history by defeating a decades-long established political incumbency. That momentum has started the reckless train of undoing at full throttle. With each instance of policy destruction and associated controversy, he is in the news. Each appearance in the media is equivalent to a Midas touch that generates gold. Not literal gold but modern-day wealth associated with trending the most. Media-driven fame and popularity boosts brand equity to unimaginable levels - this is the nature of capital that matters most in the new world. He is back in the game with a roar.

The power of his formidable touch is heightened by situating himself in the center of sensational events, constantly. He thrives on many elements of such drama - alternative facts and the resulting confusion, outlandish claims that raise eyebrows, and even immoral or unethical behavior. They are coated with lies known to travel the fastest in society, accelerated further by online media.

Many experts attempt to point out the foolhardy nature of the new presidency that is marked from the start with false or misleading statements. He uses projection effectively to hit fiercely at those that refute his approach. When projection does not work and the approach becomes shamelessly ridiculous, he resorts to deflection. The bullying nature of his rebuttals grab even more attention, fueling incessant clicks on laptops and taps on smart phones across the world. There are more eyeballs seeing his face and name every second, and that is all that matters.

As a result, the news cycles spiral out of control, daily. With it, advertising revenues on all media channels rise to unprecedented levels. The media executives face an all-new conundrum – established ethics and principles of journalism head precariously downward with every new opportunity to increase shareholder value.

TRUTHS BY PROJECTIONS

On the south lawns of the White House in the winter of 2017, many hundreds of thousands of people gather to watch the new President's inauguration ceremony. The spread of people gathered with uniformly colored hats create a sea of red. It stretches toward the Washington Monument, but not as a continuous wide mass. Halfway down the grounds sculpted with fountains and ponds with statues, the sea bifurcates like the arms of an octopus. The scattered groups then elongate haphazardly, like serpents, around the obelisk.

The numbers in the sea, the octopus and its arms, and the serpents however do not add up to a million. The fans total around three hundred thousand only. This is a disaster and totally unacceptable because the new President must be associated only with extraordinary events that can serve as fodder for his hyperbole.

The next day, his communications director projects the largest presidential inauguration crowd ever, supplanted with pictures of the event taken at angles that supports the likelihood of that stupendous success.

In this instance, the new President projects the success of his predecessor on himself.

The victory in the election was a surprise and disruption of epic proportions. But it was not a landslide. In fact, the numbers from the election commission shows that the new President lost the popular vote. Once again, this goes against the grain of everything big and grand about him. He and his advisors go on an orchestrated campaign where they continuously repeat at venues across the country that at least three million unauthorized immigrants voted illegally against him, costing him the popular vote.

This time, he projects a possibility as a reality.

Facts about illegal collaboration with a foreign government by the new President's campaign staff start to spill in the news media. The intelligence agencies corroborate such events and provide concrete data on election interference by foreign hackers.

The new President turns the table on the spillers.

He collects friendly press and media analysts in the White House briefing room. There, with the straight face and confidence of a priest sermonizing in a church, he spreads a claim that the former president wiretapped the West Village Cornelia Street apartment where the groundwork and strategy for his campaign were formulated regularly. The margins of his victory would have been significantly larger had the opponents not sneakily listened to his closely guarded and innovative campaign tactics.

This time, he projects one of his own proven follies on his predecessor.

He is accused of affairs with at least two women. While he vehemently denies any wrongdoing, a money trail links him to a Playboy model and a famous porn star. Many of his followers casually overlook this transgression as something very common among powerful men. To others who may take offence, he attempts to project on others that matter, such as one of his predecessors who had an affair while in office and was eventually impeached. When that does not work, he resorts to one of the most bizarre projections.

This defense mechanism involves his own beautiful daughter. She is married and successor of a major share of his businesses. He projects his love for beautiful woman to none other than his own daughter, claiming he would have dated her if she was not his daughter. This time, he projects in a most controversial way, attempting to normalize an adulterous behavior by bringing his daughter into the conversation.

Each projection raises countless eyebrows. They also muddy up enthusiastic discussions in most households, bars, and restaurants across the nation. The followers find reason in each projection, supporting their belief and trust in the new President. His adversaries are frustrated by the lack of accountability or a path toward clear convictions. As if when it comes to the new President's actions, anything goes.

Each projection episode, nonetheless, generates enormous controversies and continuous presence in the media. The desired effects of his newly acquired Midas touch continue unabated.

THE DEFLECTING TRUTHS

The middle class, sidelined in the modern economy, has delivered the ultimate mandate. The new President's loyalty to his voters must appear unrelenting.

After all, the supporters view him as a real estate mogul turned savior. His victory is akin to a revolution. He gave the little people a voice and vanquished the elites. The American pride is at the heart of each vote that was cast in his favor, especially across the Rust Belt.

A baker wakes up each morning at the break of dawn. Extra sticky cinnamon rolls are a signature at her bakery situated at the heart of the half-a-mile stretch of downtown. The dough must be mixed and perfectly kneaded each morning. She is inspired by her grandfather to stand on her own feet, not rely on someone else's kindness, not the social justice warriors promoted by the elites.

A farmer owns two hundred acres, passed down over three generations. His two sons have left him for jobs in the cities. He is getting older and must rely on immigrants from across the southern border to get the hard labor done. Like all working people, he wants to help others as much as he wants the border secured. After all, he says, the home should be taken care of first.

In another small town, a hairstylist is known for her humor. Her clients are loyal. They come for the dexterity of her hands and knack for suggesting the right style, for heads of hair of all kinds - full and receding, blond and black, straight like straws to curly like sheep wool. They also come for the spirited conversation that fills the air in the cozy shop with glass panes all around. She finds politicians least appealing and finds the successful businessman a big posterchild for change, caring for everyday Americans. Her clients agree wholeheartedly.

A bouncer at a nightclub is also a waiter at an upscale bistro. He considers himself just an American. His Italian, Puerto Rican, Lebanese, and Portuguese roots are important but not beyond discussions at the Thanksgiving dinner table. Liberty matters the most. And that can flourish only in a capitalist, nationalist government. What the new President stands for.

Across the spectrum of towns and farmlands in the Rust Belt, the trend continues.

In the east corner of the Belt, a fiercely entrepreneurial beauty salon owner is worried the government eyes every dollar he profits, that he is losing control. He sees synergy in how the New York tycoon-turned-President protects the proceeds from his businesses, at all costs.

In the west, a car salesman was inspired at the rallies by the then-candidate to think more about himself. He has made money for other people; it's time to revert to making a lot of it for himself. Because, America is after all a business.

An operations manager at the northern-most state in the Belt is employed at a home improvement store. He has witnessed his county's economy collapse. The new President has proven ability to recover from significant business losses – that unique trait made him a more appealing candidate.

And in the southern cities with Cajun delicacies, a student who also works part-time puts his bet on the New York businessman simply because he doesn't owe anyone anything. The new president will surely champion the common people even though he's a billionaire.

A dairy farmer from the center of the Rust Belt is the new President's favorite. He has long white hair and a chubby face with red and pink flushes on his nose and cheeks. He can easily model as Santa Claus. His business of milk and cheese products has shrunk to less than half and he is nostalgic. Sixty or seventy years back, his town had a thriving dairy industry and people had good jobs. When the new President talks about getting rid of free trade, he brings to life the waning spirit of the country. The farmer also often switches to a sarcastic tone and endorses the President's love for Russia. Each morning, when he opens the tall and creaking barn doors to milk a dwindling herd of cows, his mind ponders if Russia could nuke China and take care of the rising trade imbalance and national debt.

Many new policies the new president has promised his voters, however, are at odds with the norms. They go squarely against policies set in stone by multiple previous governments. Their acceptance by the people and their representatives in both houses of Congress needs many convincing deflections.

The new administration begins to ricochet continuously to circumvent contradictory views and competing policies by experts in the field. The threats hurled at the administration are based on traditions entrenched in the revered constitution, treasured history, and sometimes obvious scientific truths. These foundational values have to be dodged constantly.

A vast and loud army of supporters gather to validate each deflection strategy. They are buoyed by effective propaganda at rallies held regularly across the Rust Belt. Each deflection is justified by millions of social media clicks influenced by bots and humans alike. As a result, based on the generated perceptions of popularity, the President's new policies begin to stand on firmer footing. The popularity also favorably sways prominent party leaders.

For the new President, the strategy of deflections becomes a win-win. The controversies surrounding each swerve from established norms continuously arouse the news media. His name and presence remain front and center on televisions across the country and the world.

DEFLECTION - THE MUSLIMS

The new President mandates that the current axis of evil in the world be altered. This veer needs an ingenuous deflection.

One of his predecessors unceremoniously assigned three countries into that axis – Iran, Iraq, and North Korea. One of them, considered rogue and ruled by a young dictator, stands out as a non-Muslim country. It is an outlier in the new administration's direction to vehemently criticize and sanction any and all Muslim nations and their citizens. North Korea is taken off the axis. Another Muslim country will be added in its place.

Ocean City, as the name implies, is on a beach. It is on the New Jersey coastline, almost at the border of Pennsylvania. The Atlantic Sea waters are in the comfortable seventy degrees Fahrenheit more than half of the year, turning icy cold only when the deep winter sets. The long summers are hot and muggy. The sun shines bright and crisp during the winter months. All in all, it is a lovable beach town.

Locals – mostly retired couples – enjoy relaxing strolls on Main Street that leads to the well-maintained whitewashed piers. It is a classic small town with colonial buildings that flank tree-lined narrow streets with broad cobblestone sidewalks. Main Street forms the backbone of a grid of streets with coffee shops, bars and restaurants frequented by the locals and visitors alike.

At the intersection of Main Street and Pennsylvania Court that heads straight toward and ends at the sandy beach is a two-story house. Two sides of the ninety-year old house almost touch the sidewalks. The seventy-five-year-old father of five is the owner of the house along with his childhood sweetheart wife. He has always been adept in all things building and construction. Now, the strengths in his arms often fail him. A mining company executive, fixing and changing things around his favorite home has been his hobby. In his younger days, he single-handedly extended the front of the living room facing the street intersection with an L-shaped verandah. Light and dense metal netting framed with rectangular wood frames separate the verandah from the sidewalks. They bring a bit of privacy but more importantly keep mosquitoes away during the summer months of rain.

He populated the verandah with snug armchairs and sofas carefully selected by his wife. Perched comfortably in one of those, sipping coffee in the mornings and a vodka-martini in the evenings, he chats with passers-by on the sidewalks. This has been his favorite pastime, especially after his retirement. His wife, on the other hand, likes to carry her folding beach sling chair and favorite book to the beach and spend the day reading and listening to the sounds of waves and laughing children.

On a hot evening of May in 2017, the father sits on the verandah with one of his daughters-in-law. He takes special pride in how he blends very strong martini with his favorite brand of vodka and dry vermouth. He gets along with this daughter-in-law very well. She is the only one of the five who braves the level of alcohol he concocts in every glass, diluted only by the sophisticated garnish – the subtle sourness of two carefully chosen olives from a collection he orders directly from a farm in Italy. She is also the daughter of a Sri Lankan immigrant, the only one who is not a Caucasian.

As the martini kicks in, the effect somewhat exacerbated by the warm and humid still air, he diverts their conversation to a book he had finished reading early that day. He starts off by acknowledging that she and her parents are Hindus and he respects that religion, especially the unique doctrine that one can only be a born Hindu. Christianity and Islam, on the other hand, invite religious conversion. Many invasions and wars have occurred in history as a result of this intent. The book offers multiple, detailed, and disturbing details of how such a religious invasion has begun in his country.

The daughter-in-law shifts in her chair with discomfort, knowing where the conversation may be going, as he continues his monologue. Ruthless killings and terrorist activities by Muslim organizations like Al Qaeda and ISIL aren't being condemned enough by Muslim nations. He stops to check her reaction and is pleased to see her nod in agreement.

The new President is implementing a ban on Muslims, he will stop their silent invasion of the country. He is going a bit too far – she surmises quietly – the notion of stereotyping all Muslims to be of one kind. She contemplates an interruption and a challenge to the picture of hate and division her father-in-law continues to paint. She decides against it as he begins to slowly sound like a fanatic. She asks for another drink just to break the one-sided conversation. He grins wide like the loving dad he always is, praises her grit and his martini alike, and hurries back to the bar.

The book, whichever one he may have read, and she does not want to know which one it is, has reinforced his view of the grave threats the nation faces. Those same views stood as a rock behind his decision last year to vote for the new President.

As the father returns, this time with some extra olive and lime garnish in the drinks, his wife joins them. She does not like martini, prefers instead a glass of South African Cabernet, from the wineries of Stellenbosch near Cape Town she visited last winter. She and the daughter-in-law change the conversation to activities their two grandchildren are beginning to excel in, both at school and extracurricular.

A man in his sixties is the British author of the book the father read. Dressed in his best tuxedo, he is seated in the White House West Wing, waiting to meet members of the new President's administration.

A film of sweat shines on his bald head, some trickling down through the black curly hair on the sides and back of his head. His glasses are round, like those of John Lennon's and he sports a French beard, but without the moustache. He is a Muslim and wears his beard like one. And that is where his allegiance to the religion ends.

He flew in just the previous day from London, in first class, paid for by the White House administration. But he did not sleep at all, as is the case for him on all long-haul flights. He waits uncomfortably seated in an upright wooden chair with no cushions situated in front of a tall and daunting door with a small desk and a petit secretary next to it. A few minutes pass by. The woman on the desk finally raises her head and calls his name. She advises him that his meeting will begin promptly in fifteen minutes and asks him to settle and relax in the adjoining lounge. He feels the jet lag creep in. He stands up, pulls the handkerchief out of his trouser pocket, and wipes the sweat off. He asks the secretary to fetch him a double shot of espresso.

He has been outcasted by many leaders of his own religion – including those in the axis of evil - because of his radical views that attack the fundamentalism of the Mullahs and Ayatollahs. The interpretations propagated by the British author can be effective deflections for anti-Muslim policies, especially to eliminate any taints of racism. Such scholastically founded opinions, especially by a well-known Cambridge-educated author, have attracted the new administration and the President himself. It is very likely he will be appointed a role in the foreign relations office, to develop future policies related to Muslim countries. One of his first assignments would be to install a third Muslim country into the axis of evil.

DEFLECTION – THE CHINESE

The city of Shenzhen in the Chinese province of Guangdong is very colorful. But, rather incongruently. Likely a result of disjointed social and economic cultures slapped together.

The green ambiance of the city oozes from lines of neatly planted Lychee and Mango trees. Under the lush leafy foliage, especially on neon-lit streets, greedy pimps and their lecherous customers play hide and seek.

Blood-red Bougainvillea creep up in glorious abundance on walls of tall buildings in the bustling metropolis and the well-planned, spacious suburbs. In those government-built structures live hard-working families constrained in multiple dimensions. Numerous hours spent toiling and away from home does not supplant the lack of funds in their bank accounts or grow the limited space in their homes. The communist government's legacy one-child policy forces subdued conjugality limiting growth of families.

The cityscape is vibrant with shades of modernism and capitalism. A result of rapid reform and open trade policies and generous influx of foreign investment, it has ascended to become a technology hub rivaling Silicon Valley in California. Men and women of the city dress formally and many speak English well, thanks to the influence of and proximity to Hong Kong, a British colony for over fifteen decades.

The general manager of a computer networking hardware company in Silicon Valley is on his thirty-seventh visit to the intriguing city. After his preferred direct San Francisco-to-Hong Kong fourteen-hour flight, he hops into a company-arranged limousine. He stretches and unwinds and sinks into the comfort of the wide and soft leather seat. It is approximately a two-hour-ride to Shenzhen, on winding roads through lush tropical greens.

He always insists on Hong Kong as a transit point. After a week of spicy Chinese food, that Shenzhen is known for, he likes to enjoy an evening in Kowloon. This urban area, that is also a peninsula, overlooks the spectacularly lit silhouette of tall, jagged hills and glass-covered skyscrapers off the harbor. A medium-cooked burger with a garnish of crispy bacon and melted blue cheese at his favorite restaurant that feature a karaoke of classic Creedence Clearwater Revival and Fleetwood Mac songs – the experience always makes his trip complete.

On the way to Shenzhen, the limousine makes its routine stop at the border into mainland China. The general manager waits impatiently as the customs and immigration officers inspect each vehicle and occupants carefully. He opens his laptop and contemplates a plan for the next day.

He looks forward to an informal meeting in the morning; his trained fingers type notes straight from this strategically thinking mind. Over coffee at a bustling Starbucks at the center of the city, he will sit shoulder-to-shoulder with his customer-turned friend. He is a senior executive at China's largest and the world's second largest networking equipment company, head-quartered in Shenzhen. The general manager will extract vital inside information from his US-educated friend so that his presentation to a broader audience later in the afternoon is correctly positioned and targeted.

The general manager's Silicon Valley company enjoys north of twenty million dollars in annual revenue from the Chinese company. New business deals are a must to drive a much-needed fifteen percent revenue growth in the next two years. New products being developed by the hard-working engineers in Shenzhen will compete fiercely against similar products already sold by the world's number one networking equipment company, based in the US. And this company is also his customer. And that gives him a unique distinction – he is more sought after by the executives of the Chinese company.

What he knows and says is highly valued and everyone attending his meetings in Shenzhen will listen very intently. At the same coffee shop the following day after the meeting, he knows that his Chinese friend will look up to him wanting to understand how best to compete against the US-based behemoth respected throughout the world for innovation.

The five-star Intercontinental Hotel in the northern corner of the city is opulent on all fronts, beginning with the lush welcoming red carpets with golden dragons and beautiful smiling attendants at the grand entrance. The general manager's suite includes a bathtub uniquely situated in the middle of the room, between the king-sized bed and an embarrassingly large and ornate desk. A warm bath prior to sinking into the silky softness of the bed will ensure much-needed sound sleep. In the oval-shaped bath overfilled with rich foam, he lies naked, as if floating in the clouds.

His mind is occupied fully - contemplating a full-proof strategy to win new business at all cost. He will explain his silicon product architecture in excruciating detail, to impress them. The zeal is however mixed with significant apprehension. Some of the deep knowhow about his company's prized intellectual property will be transferred during his presentations. The knowledge can be utilized by a wholly owned subsidiary of the Chinese company to build a product that competes against his. That is the risk of doing business in China, he surmises, as he closes his tired eyes and dims the lights in the room with a remote.

Across the globe, in Washington DC, a few members of the new President's administration brave the traffic toward 1600 Pennsylvania Avenue NW. Among them are two foreign policy advisors; one is a technocrat who has lived in Beijing for several years, and the other is an expert in Chinese cultural and economic affairs. The two stayed up till the early hours of the morning, researching Chinese government tactics to shape public opinion and curb external competition to foster the growth of local companies.

At 10 AM sharp, the Chief Secretary steps into a meeting room in the West Wing of the White House. He does not waste a minute; immediately and abruptly plunging into controversy. The topic is about waging an intense and prolonged trade war against China. The progress and dominance of the rising Asian power must be curbed by stopping intellectual property theft.

China also wields significant influence over North Korea and the latter's ability to be a constant nuclear threat to the United States. The multiple generations of dictators in North Korea have led puppet regimes controlled by China. To be able to wage a trade war against China, North Korea must first be pulled out of the axis of evil, the Chief Secretary continues. The President must strike cordial terms with the youngest North Korean dictator. The thirty-three-year-old leader – for a change – must lean on the United States, not China.

Everyone in the West Wing meeting room acknowledges the risks of waging a trade war with the most important and powerful trading partner. This also means aligning interests with a ruthless dictator known to have severely decapitated or murdered Americans.

Reactions in the public arising out of such controversial policies and initiatives must be deflected. An energetic young official suggests that the plight of voters in the Rust Belt can be utilized to create effective deflections. After all, so many of the manufacturing jobs have shifted to China. They can be promptly returned to the homeland with the right set of trade policies. So can the plight of the farmers in the Mid-West be eradicated, adds another official. The right set of tariffs on goods imported from China will boost export of crops and agricultural goods at prices that support the necessary profit margins farmers want, and of course the good old American way of life. Such noble initiatives to eradicate the plight of the middle class will hold the attention of the media. The dangers posed by the trade wars will largely go unnoticed, especially by the President's base of supporters.

The President flirts with many new ideas, often playing with fire, bordering on instigating the enemy to shoot highly destructive missiles and starting the next World War. Over the next few months, the policies and media reactions with all things related to China go into a tailspin. The inexperienced North Korean dictator's hunger for worldwide attention is whetted with pageantry. He is enticed into a game of political flirtation, just to get China upset and jealous. Meanwhile the President's staunch supporters in the Rust Belt and the Mid-West rejoice at the prospects of an impending surge in the number of jobs and profits.

DEFLECTION –
THE RUSSIANS

The genesis of this deflection occurs at the end of the summer of 2015. The presidential campaigns are heating up, the rhetoric is divisive. The moods at rallies are often on the verge of violent eruption.

A twenty-nine-year old Russian woman moves to the United States.

She enrolls as a graduate student in International Relations at a University in Washington, D.C. She experiences the rage among voters. Over the following two years, she attends classes sporadically and barely manages passing grades.

The country begins to break apart into two as deeply partisan groups engage in fiery policy debates. On most evenings, the Russian woman leaves the University campus and stealthily walks the affluent neighborhoods.

Five blocks down from campus, she enters the tree-lined sidewalks of Palisades. Her destination is one of the apartments among many in a row of brown and red brick buildings. The century-old regal structures have freshly painted white doors, windows and curved eaves that support ash-gray tiled roofs.

A flight of seven stairs leads up from the sidewalk to a small verandah and plush doormat. At the ring of the bell, the door is opened promptly by a butler. She greets him, walks in through the entryway, straight toward the closet as she takes off her heavy fur coat.

The tastefully decorated apartment has high cathedral ceilings. The tall French windows adorn very long moss green and crimson-red drapes. The carefully folded fabric falls gracefully from the ceilings to the ivory marble floors decorated with Persian carpets and ornate French furniture. There, in the living room, and sometimes in the bedroom, she works with many operatives to push the Russian agenda, to influence the results of the upcoming election.

On some weekends however, she stays behind at the University. With students in their meagerly furnished dormitories, she unwinds and gets drunk. She brags about her upbringing in rural Siberia and her love for guns. On wilder evenings, drinks get mixed with cocaine and her mention of contacts in the Russian government catches the attention of law enforcement.

Her roots are in the heartland of Siberia where a home without a rifle is rare. The swampy coniferous forests between the tundra and steppes are always covered with snow. She grew up there, hunting with guns her father introduced her to. Her fixation with the National Rifle Association (NRA) and the charter it promotes in the United States is therefore most natural to her. While still a high school student, she proposed to the Russian government that the United States Republican Party's interests can be aligned better with those of Russia, through the NRA.

Her strong affiliation with the NRA and distinctively rustic personality makes her a sought-after woman among a few right-wing activists. To one staunch republican from South Dakota, she is like the fierce winds of the tundra and he falls for her. Using his influence, she dodges serious attention of investigators and possible arrest.

The University campus includes a main quadrangle surrounded by academic buildings, a 5,000-seat arena, and an outdoor Amphitheatre. Her graduation at the Amphitheatre is attended by some of the Russian operatives from the Palisades apartment and members of the NRA. Her invitation references them simply as friends and family.

The winds are blowing favorably in the highly charged political scene. After graduation, instead of returning to Russia, she extends her visa and moves in with her Republican boyfriend.

Later that winter, she is invited to the newly elected president's inauguration ball. There, on the grounds of the White House, she is noticed mingling with Russian oligarchs. The next morning, the FBI raids her apartment.

On the eve of half a year since the new President assumed office and moved to the White House, a Russian spy is convicted.

An experienced magistrate judge in the District Court for the District of Columbia files charges: conspiring to act as an unregistered foreign agent of the Russian state. The intent to study International Relations at an esteemed American University was after all a veneer.

The blonde-haired, twenty-nine-year-old spy with sharp slanting eyes and a prominent manly chin sits confidently by her attorney, facing the judge. Her alleged Republican boyfriend, who has also been charged by another court in South Dakota, is not by her side. She stares intently at the judge, and brags about her unique approach to influence the course of democracy in the world. She has used her love for guns to infiltrate United States politics, leveraging the right wing's reliance on the NRA. The charges are grave; she is sentenced to eighteen months in prison.

The voters that propelled the New York businessman to the office of the Presidency want nationalism back. Foreign policy advisors develop a radical new strategy to fight globalism. The Russian spy is transformed to a pawn in that larger game.

She contends confidently that the seeds she planted to boost the resurgence of nationalism and need for guns in the country have been effective in electing the new government. Her voice from behind bars in a prison cell in Florida goes unheard. Her role is diminished as superfluous because nationalism and gun culture in the country go hand-in-hand and are etched in the Second Amendment of the Constitution. Soon, she fades into oblivion.

The fate of the nations of the world are intertwined, economically, politically, and most recently with climate change. Globalism is here to stay; it cannot be denied; even the President gets it. To implement a purely US-focused nationalist agenda, all predicaments with other countries need to be eliminated or deflected.

The White House concludes that the United States needs a new powerful ally to whom all responsibilities related to globalism can be shifted. For example, the heavy burden of maintaining the balance of powers across the world must be relinquished. Decades-old policies and initiatives related to wars and military influence must be taken off the administration's charter.

The advisors direct the President to request Russia to take on that role, especially in the most sensitive areas of the world such as the middle east. Since the Kremlin commissioned the spy and unleashed her into the center of the election frenzy, the Russian President has been waiting for the opportunity to direct affairs in the world stage like never before. The move in the White House is a significant step toward the resurgence of Russia as a superpower.

Sanctions have been imposed against Russia unanimously by both parties in both houses of Congress to counter the threat of election interference. These must now be retracted. Maneuvering through the controversies that will arise will need a whole new set of deflections.

At the next G7 and United Nations summits, the President unleashes trade wars against Germany and Canada. He threatens to pull out of the NATO and the Climate Agreement. He rejects the Iran Nuclear deal. He rejects the idea of Russian interference in the elections that placed him in the highest office. He ignores the annexation of Crimea by Russia and presses that Russia be allowed back into the G8.

World leaders are confused. They struggle to find the new leader among them, with the United States seeming to go astray. The Russians, in the meantime, extend their reach into the middle east, starting with significant military presence in Syria and a new arms-deal with Iran.

The outrageous nature of the new policies seems to aggravate one faction of the press and media. The other recognizes them as brave, game-changing, and much needed. This drives even deeper wedges in the society, causing factions to move farther apart. The leaders of the social media companies double down on freedom of speech as the reason to allow all forms of deeply partisan communication.

There are many discords between the television media companies that stand for left- and right-wing policies. A vital common thread however goes unnoticed by the common people – that there are now significantly more eyeballs on the screens and therefore more money to be made from advertisement revenues. The top executives of these companies enjoy unexpected windfalls. They let the conflicts and arguments on their shows spiral out of bound. As a result, the Midas touch of the President gets further primed to deliver a surge in his net worth.

INTERLUDE II:
THE UNBENDABLE TRUTHS

The clock on the wall strikes eleven times. The President tosses and turns alone. The bed in the master suite in the southwest corner of the White House is not comfortable enough. He has been catapulted, albeit pleasantly, beyond his wildest imagination - from the New York City penthouse to the bedroom where Lincoln and Roosevelt once slept. From being a controversial hero of a prime-time reality TV show into presidential stardom.

Outside the window, the two hundred-year-old Jackson Magnolia leans precariously - the weight of the collecting snow on the leaves and branches bogging it down.

Another impatient thirty minutes go by. Finally, sleep and silence shroud the beige colored room. The stark black furniture is barely visible. Under his eyelids, below a tense and creased forehead, a frightful dream takes shape.

The ceiling is white and bland. Ornamental crown moldings flank each side, breaking the monotony. Slowly, the flat dull surface begins to thaw, and a frightening vision appears. Dark storm clouds move at breakneck speed over fields of crops. Each long stem holding precious produce stands frozen. Actually, they hang upside down and below a layer of pitch-dark soil that forms on the surface of the melting ceiling.

The produce transforms to the much sought-after form of golden harvest. Swift jets of summer breeze constantly nurture the crops, fostering viral growth. In the inverted world of his dream, the harvest transforms to many gleaming streams. They flow rapidly through a maze of trenches. These channels are underground, below the dark soil. At the end of the trenches, the surreal flows transform a final time. They become currency bills or bars of gold – things that can be touched, occupy space, and have weight. Their properties are unbreakable truths ingrained in the laws of physics and the mathematical preciseness of finance and economics.

This world that takes shape in his dream is completely disassociated from his home base and platform. The loud roars of his loyal supporters in rallies go silent. The incessant clicks that like and share posts to promote favorable right-wing opinions cease to operate. The numerous bots that boost the popularity of his messages are frozen. Instead of proliferating rapidly, his communication becomes sluggish; the words fall into quicksand and drown.

In this deep underground inverted world above the ceiling of his bedroom, the President shudders and then wonders. Can he create new truths there? Can the established truths ingrained in the sciences of that world be bent?

A few uncomfortable minutes pass. A single piercing eye appears. Its sight, like the effect of Medusa, begins to further numb the President. His body begins to rise from the bed, uncontrollably. He grabs the mattress and sheets, desperately. He resists the upward movement in vain.

The eye, now becoming more expressive, swiftly leads him through the dark soil and melted ceiling, into the trenches. With a smirk, it points the President to the mouths of two tunnels. Each of them is a money trail. They represent a continuum from the past he has lived to the destiny he is seeking, the potential returns from his Midas touch. In contrast to the dark bedroom and the soil they just traversed, the trails are bright, as if the sun is shining through them.

The first trail leads back to his ancestors. This is where the genesis of his affluence is. His character and strategies for wealth creation and expansion evolve from there.

The far end of the second trail holds records of the source of his current net worth. In a pitch-black vault secured firmly to surrounding walls and the ground are his liquid assets. This is a likely destination for all viral wealth to be generated by his Midas touch - the trivial but fundamental intent of the wild journey to the White House.

The light from the tunnels is now blindingly bright. He can barely see the fast-moving eye but begins to hear sounds. As if the silent grin he observed in the eye has now turned into loud and disconcerting laughter.

As he stands, contemplating a step forward into one of the trails, he experiences an unnerving loneliness. The social media-based tactics that brought him to the White House have become irrelevant. This throws a curveball, making his highly successful approach thus far untenable. The very foundation of his presidential quest is now in jeopardy.

THE ANCESTRAL
MONEY TRAIL

The first trail runs at the base of a perfectly square tunnel. A revealing set of events lie along its length. They spotlight the tactics employed to boost wealth, spanning three generations, one building on the other. The very foundation of the President's family dealings in the hospitality and real estate industries emerge from there.

The strategies - some genius with foresight and others bordering on vice and fraud – began more than a century ago. The roving eye, now situated on the flat ceiling of the tunnel, casts its powerful vision; the surroundings transform to black and white. It takes the President back in time, like the Ghosts of Christmases Past, Present and Future in the movie based on Dickens' book. He is swooped through the tunnel, right to the end. To the period before the gold rush of the northwest frontier, the pursuits of his grandfather, where it all began.

PART 1

He is a thin but hardworking thirteen-year old lad, in the village of Kallstadt in Germany. The winemaking heritage in the area dates back all the way to the Roman times. He, however, detests alcohol. So, he apprentices as a barber in contrast to the norm. He slogs seven days a week, wielding a pair of scissors skillfully, morning to evening, for three years.

One evening he sits down to ponder his future. At the edge of the village, the sun sinks behind the Pfälzerwald forest throwing orange hues on the lower slopes of the Haardt Mountains on the other side. There isn't enough business in Kallstadt to earn a living. The imperial German army will soon enlist him for mandatory service. This isn't his destiny.

Three evenings later, in the darkness of the night, he leaves a note for his mother and boards a ship bound for New York. He is only sixteen when he arrives alone as the ship with very tall sails docks on a crowded pier by the Statue of Liberty.

The US immigration office classifies him as illegal for

escaping military service in his home country. Non-the-less, he is allowed to enter the land of immigrants and opportunities.

The young boy with a stained leather suitcase, a tattered thickly lined green suede jacket, and a far-fetched dream is welcomed by one of his sisters. She is settled in a German-speaking neighborhood situated in the New York metropoli-tan. There, the next day, he finds a friendly German-speaking employer, and starts to earn as a barber. He continues so for the next six years, saving every cent he can and learning to speak English fluently.

The President's first ancestral property in the United States of America is realized in Seattle. His twenty-two-year-old grandfather moves from New York City to the thriving city of the northwest. The goal is to open a restaurant using up all his life savings. He strategically selects a location on Washington Street, what is also called 'the line". It includes an assortment of casinos and saloons and in their midst, discretely placed brothels.

The intent to acquire a fortune in gold and silver soon be-comes overwhelming. He sells his restaurant for a moder-ate sum and moves to the emerging mining town of Monte Cristo in Snohomish county, north of Seattle. With other miners, he joins the gold rush. He finds that his weak con-stitution isn't suitable for the laborious job, returns to Seattle and opens another restaurant, this time on Cherry Street.

159

The lure of the Yukon gold rush cannot hold him back, he must be amid the action, among peers aggressively driven by the lure of a windfall. He travels to the Klondike region and the famous White Horse route; the intent this time is not to mine, but mine the miners.

While on the Dead Horse Trial, he and a fellow miner see an opportunity as they watch frustrated travelers whip their horses to death. They open the Arctic restaurant in a tent. It grows quickly to a sea of tents. Besides fine dining and lodging, the specialty is "rooms for ladies". The private rooms include beds and scales for measuring gold dust. The frequent and popular dish is cheaply procured – it is freshly slaughtered horse meat.

When the one hundred- and eleven-mile White Pass and Yukon Route railroad is completed to connect Skagway in Alaska to White Horse in Yukon, he and his mining partner build and open the White Horse Restaurant and Inn. Trains bring tourists from far and wide and with that, more unneeded attention. Vices can no longer be carried on discreetly; the local government announces suppression of prostitution, gambling, and liquor. He senses the impending threat to his restaurant and hotel business and promptly sells his share to his partner and leaves Yukon.

A wealthy man, commanding a net worth of 80,000 deutsche marks, he returns to Kallstadt and marries. He soon returns to New York and works as a barber and a hotel manager. Later, his ability to visit his home country and village is extinguished by the German government as he is expelled for dodging military service.

When World War 1 rages, he keeps a low profile to avoid confronting widespread anti-German sentiments across New York. When the war ends, his net worth is about thirty thousand dollars. He plants the seed of a real estate business by owning a two story, seven room home in Queens, and five vacant lots in other New York city boroughs.

Thanks to the widespread pursuits for wealth in Seattle and the northwest, the Klondike region and the boroughs of New York, the neurons in his brain learned forever many vital tricks of the trade. They are to be passed on to his descendants, but most prominently to his grandson.

The President considers the wealth assembled by his grandfather – a mere $30,000; it is meagre by his standards even after adjusting to present value. But then, he died young and suddenly, didn't get to earn to his full potential.

The pursuits of the President's grandfather from the small and almost unknown village of Kallstadt marks the beginning of a slow but certain emergence of real estate wealth and business prowess. The modest prosperity is drawn from businesses built on pure soil, brick, and mortar, albeit somewhat obscure and low-key means by the President's standards. He winks with a strange mix of disappointment and pride.

On the retreat back through the trail in the square tunnel, he stops midway. Tinges of brown and orange color begin to appear in the white, gray, and black surroundings. The colors emanating from the mysterious eye projects an era of early modernism, post-World War II. This is the time of his handsome and thrifty father.

The mastery of leveraged investments and the ability to turn government regulations and tax codes upside down to benefit fiscally are acquired here. Combined with a knack to utilize inflections, the father proves to be a shrewd business-man. Down the length of this trail on the way back to the bedroom in the master suite of the White House, these skills are to be passed on to the President, along with enormous wealth as loans, bailout money, and gifts.

PART 2

Inside a modest two-story home in the Woodhaven neigh-borhood of Queens, a young boy struggles with the sudden death of his father from the Spanish Flu. Every night, he is plagued by nightmares about the epidemic and its devastat-ing impact across the world. His desire to escape the grief is intense. From the bedroom window, he observes cobble-stone streets being widened for newfangled automobiles. His sixteen-year-old brain latches onto the vision to get into construction. With help from his mother who acts as his adult business partner and utilizing some of his father's money, he begins to build garages for the emerging mode of transportation. The neighbors and his clients agree that his innate talent for building is impressive.

When the Great Depression of 1929 sets in, he notices the strong desire among his neighbors to save every cent. He opens a supermarket where customers serve themselves and save, making it an instant hit. He becomes the talk of the town in Woodhaven, but he maintains a low profile.

As the world prepares to see the end of World War II, the forward thinker takes out loans to build middle-income housing for returning servicemen. They would need a fresh start with their families. The thousands of homes in sturdy brick rental towers that he builds over a decade changes the face of Brooklyn and Queens. He also makes a mark along the East Coast, building barracks and garden apartments near major shipyards for returning navy personnel.

And when the next recession sets in, he buys up apartment buildings from others who struggles to keep them. In a quiet way, he expands his real estate presence significantly. His family, now growing in size, moves to a large Tudor-style house in the most affluent neighborhood of Queens. But they live frugally, oblivious of the rapidly growing family wealth. None of them realize or appreciate his business savviness, especially the unique knack to see the future and act at the right time.

When many of his Jewish tenants show discomfort at the owner being a German, especially when World War II rages, he begins to claim Swedish origin. Standing six feet tall and with his handsome face sporting a black bushy moustache and a wide forehead with a receding hairline, he can easily pass off as a descendent of the ingenious Sami people of the northern Nordic lands.

Along the way as he expands his net worth to almost a billion dollars, he exploits loopholes in federal housing rules and tax codes to the maximum. One of his sons, that he considers highly talented, begins to assist him in his business. The dashing young man is almost the same height as his father. Above a prominent chin and a sharp nose flanked by bushy eyebrows like that of his father is a full head of blonde hair that covers most of his forehead. He has just returned with a business degree from the Wharton School in Pennsylvania. The son develops ideas that help them take profit levels in some of the later projects to previously unseen levels. They resort to profiteering by overestimating construction costs and paying inflated amounts for construction equipment. A loophole allows them to be both the builder and the supplier of construction equipment to the builder. Using another gap in regulations, they are able to buy land and lease long term for an exorbitant amount. They use large loans to lease the same land to build apartments. They become masters at fooling the financial systems designed by naïve and unsuspecting government officials.

In return for the significant boost in net worth that resulted from tactics that his son architected, the father gifts and loans over $400M over his lifetime. Gifts are sometimes masqueraded as shares in his business sold well below their purchase price. The son benefits from tax write-offs.

The swashbuckling son ventures into more glamorous turfs such as branding the family's name and logo. The need for fame and recognition that boosts brand equity takes center stage. To the delight of his proud father, he also begins to manipulate the media to heighten the success of their fresh real estate pursuits in Manhattan.

Between the grandfather and the father, the net worth of the family increased more than ten thousand times. The real estate business in the Queens and Brooklyn boroughs of New York takes a strong and indelible footing. The subtle strain of vice persists across the two generations, transitioning from exploitation of human lust to more complex loopholes in government rules and tax codes. The family also discards its true German heritage and falsely adopts a new one to benefit business.

The eye leading the President is his dreams is now planted on the right wall of the tunnel; it blinks multiple times. As if from continuous strikes of lighting from the periphery of the eye, the entire tunnel flickers in unison. An important streak of character develops in this mid-section of the trail – that of skillfully creating and delivering lies to boost personal wealth. The President droops from the weight of the prudence just acquired. He drifts back to the present where many of the tactics of wealth creation formulated in this section of the trail begin to explode.

The third part of the trail belongs to the President and his own business pursuits. It is the most significant as the family name and logo become recognized worldwide. The wide-open eye leads him to this portion of the tunnel, bright with all colors present. The adventurous journey to the White House commences, drawing from key lessons learned from his two nearest ancestors.

The overarching principle learned is that in business dealings personal opinions and positions should be fungible in the interest of wealth creation. If the tenant is a Jew during World War II, the landlord should rather be of Swedish origin than German. That is the decree from his father. If serving one's country comes in the way of starting a lucrative business, like his grandfather, avoiding a military draft makes perfect sense. If government regulations and tax laws allow inflation and deflation of costs and assets to derive windfall profits, it is plain smart - as his father would smile and preach - to take advantage of such loopholes. Similarly, if the vices of men – the lure of sex or money or the inhuman slaughtering of weak horses – open opportunities for business and profits, they should be exploited. Just like his grandfather did to bootstrap a successful business from almost nothing. Finally, incessant hard work and complete focus on business success must be skillfully applied in combination with tactics that capitalize changing social and economic conditions. This created many instances of massive payouts for his father.

The President ingrains each of the above traits into his character, etched firmly like in stone.

PART 3

He starts like his father in real estate, only wanting to extend the reach of his properties to adjacent boroughs. But ends up rather differently.

The initial intent to expand real estate-based wealth aggressively using the platforms of his ancestors – based on pure soil, brick, and mortar - runs into multiple hurtful bankruptcies. The failures compel a morphosis into more lucrative methods that harness money from controversies and popularity. The recipe from his ancestors gets a new ingredient – hyperbole hemmed with a dose of bullying and merciless bending of truths. As a result, a unique and unprecedented path emerges that leads the businessman like a deluging unstoppable river all the way into the White House.

At the onset, he takes a loan from his father. His intent is to replicate the success of his father in Queens and Bronx. He will do so in the more glamorous Manhattan. Like his father, he builds condominiums, apartments and local government-backed housing and even makes plans for a shopping complex on the west side of the borough. Unlike his father, the sizes of the properties he builds are significantly larger, so he resorts to taking massive loans and making leveraged investments. Somewhat like his grandfather but on a significantly more lavish scale, he builds and purchases luxury hotels and casinos. But unlike both his ancestors, he fails to see an impending downturn in business conditions and adjust to come out unscathed. The recession of the 1980s hits him hard and results in many bankruptcy filings.

He does not give up. He convinces his current lenders to keep him afloat. He manages to coax the executives at a new and aspiring foreign bank to loan him huge sums, effectively bail him out. An initial public offering of a portion of his business, significant boost in net worth of a Wall Street building he bought and renovated, and a huge sum he inherits when his father dies gives him a cushion and a launch pad.

For the next phase of his growth strategy, he utilizes fame to boost brand equity. Initially, he follows conventional methods of promoting his name and personality as a symbol of luxury and quality. Later, when his name recognition skyrockets – thanks to a hit reality TV show where he is the star - he pivots to a different strategy. The number of iconic buildings flaunting his name and brand increase substantially, worldwide. Instead of building properties, he resorts to licensing his brand and logo to other builders. He creates and promotes the fake impression that he owns the iconic monuments across the world. None-the-less, the media bites on his stories; they further boost his recognition and perceived net worth.

His fortune is now in excess of three billion dollars. But it isn't sufficient. It is only three times that of his father who had boosted it to more than ten thousand times compared to his grandfather. He exaggerates his brand value by a hundred times, but the financial pundits reject that claim. On the Forbes List of billionaires, he is nowhere close to being on the top.

The tunnel begins to dim rapidly as the lids lower to render the roving eye more than half shut. The President picks up pace as he treads the final portion of the trail back to the White House bedroom and the upside-down world on the ceiling. Now that he is the most powerful man on the planet, he wonders how much his brand value may have appreciated.

THE MONEY TRAIL TO THE VAULT

The mouth of this trail is built with red bricks. The pyramid triangle shape is a perfect masonic symbol. The all-seeing eye at the center is wide open, the glint is protective. The President ignores the caring look that feels like from his mother's gentle face. He walks at his usual fast pace through the tunnel. A few twists and turns and then he jumps across a narrow drain with algae-ridden flowing water. The trail ends abruptly inside 60 Wall Street. It is a 47-story skyscraper in the heart of the Financial District.

The location is very familiar to the President, from his days as a fledgling businessman under the coaching of his father wanting to make a mark in the elite circles of Manhattan.

The building used to house ambitious executives and bankers of a German bank that set up its US headquarters in Lower Manhattan to compete head-to-head with American banks in their own backyard. With some of them, his very close friends, he had spent countless hours on luxurious golf courses in New Jersey, Florida, and Scotland.

Etched in sophisticated bank documents in the deep insides of the multi-national institution lies dormant a trove of hidden data about his personal finances and business dealings. Preserved like the carefully laid skeletons in ossuaries, not to be touched or moved. They can expose the President's true performance to date as a businessman. If the financial elites get their hands on the bank ledgers that record each transaction with his name, the tally may add up to a net worth significantly less than the value of three billion dollars he has been touting. Ever since he got elected, they have been after the ledgers trying to link him to fraud by filing many lawsuits in the powerful courts of the Southern District of New York.

At the entrance of 60 Wall Street, he stands at one end of a long corridor. The walls and floor are festooned with expensive Calcutta Gold marble, the subtle but distinct light gray and gold veins in the expensive stone stretch along the length of the floor.

The tower was designed by famed architects to fit its surroundings with a postmodern and neoclassical look. It is surrounded by slim pre-World War II towers, making a prominent impact on the Lower Manhattan skyline. The lobby has an entrance to the Wall Street subway station on the IRT Broadway–Seventh Avenue Line.

The wall on the east side of the corridor is lined with countless elevator doors. One of them opens with a gentle ding. The President steps in.

The elevator ascends quickly and stops at the entrance on the 46th floor. It overlooks the familiar East River. He rushes out of the elevator and immediately notices that the opulence of the surroundings he has been used to is rapidly fading. Instinctively, he proceeds toward where the offices of the senior-most bank executives are. Many of them have been his trusted friends and golf-buddies over the years.

The first corner office is that of the chief executive of the bank. The second is that of the chief executive's immediate junior and subsequently his successor. The third is that of the president's personal banker. The bank's operation ran from those offices. They symbolized the vaulting ambition of the foreign bank.

Wall-to-wall glass windows span across the three offices. They look upon spectacular views of the saltwater tidal estuary that connects Upper New York Bay on its south end to Long Island Sound on its north end.

Lately, the bank has taken a downward spiral, hit by multiple regulatory and politically motivated investigations. The

President, with his past dealings with the bank, is at the center of many allegations. As a result, each office is now empty.

Stacks of brown boxes are lined up along the walls. Heaps of papers in them contain many trails of the aggressive initiatives by bank executives that sought meteoric rise in both wealth and their own personal standings. Some strains on those trails carry data about the President's true net worth, how he built his wealth and who he did business with. In other words, they contain financial statements and ledgers with vital information about transactions concerning the President.

The motherly compassion projected by the eye surfaces once again to the chagrin of the President, this time by the door of the first office. He always thought his mother was not a fit in his father's household; her personality was too weak. She failed to be there for him when he was a toddler and most needed her caring. She had no interest in participating in her husband's business dealings or the charities he contributed to for building goodwill. He always detested the vulnerability that he felt cast upon him by her proximity.

The lamps light up in the office. Time rolls back. It is 2011. The CEO of the German bank is in his last few months holding that title. The lean shoulders under a perfectly shaped bald head are burdened heavily. He seems unable to carry his tall stature with confidence anymore; he walks with a hunch. He badly needs a recourse for the next phase of his life. He approves another huge loan to the New York businessman. When the real-estate bubble burst in 2008, the businessman not only defaulted on previous loans from the bank but also litigated against the bank blaming it for the crisis itself. None of that mattered. A loan in excess of $550 million gets approved.

The occupant in the next office will only further enhance the bank's striking relationship with the businessman. The successor to the previous CEO appears slowly in the dimly lit room as time progresses to 2013. He is perched forward as if eager to meet the businessman. His distinctly brown-skinned young face is resting on the cupped palm of his right hand. Under the glass desk, the crisply ironed blue woolen trousers and fawn-colored Italian-made shoes emphasize his constant desire to look smart. A middle-aged lady, the businessman's personal banker, steps into the office. Together, the three head to the businessman's tower in Manhattan. Over lunch that includes the most expensive Maine lobster and fresh Japanese tuna, the brown-skinned executive browses over financial documents that the personal banker presents. He admires the businessman's relatively low levels of debt. He approves multiple loans instantly to allow the businessman to convert an old post office building into a luxury hotel in Washington D.C. and rebuild an ailing golf course in Miami.

The caring look in the eye begins to fade, and with it the light from the afternoon sun that becomes obscured by dark clouds. The President is transported back to the gloomy present. The rooms and corridors are once again empty. The number of brown boxes stacked up along the walls have now doubled. Like a procession of ants, they lead the President back to the elevator.

The door shuts quickly before the elevator starts its rapid descent toward the underground vault. There, in a pitch-black iron box with sophisticated locks are his tangible assets in cash and gold. About forty flights down, the lift stops unexpectedly.

The door opens to a trading floor. More brown boxes lead the way to empty seats in trading stations where the computer screens are black. A large window with thick glass is pushed open. Sound carries over with a sudden gust of wind, from the nearby Full Shilling pub. Over beers, the junior traders lament betting on inflated assets and discuss opportunities at competing banks.

Older and richer traders are at Cipriani on Wall Street, where the famous Bellini cocktails are served in wood-paneled rooms. The exaggerated net worth of the New York businessman takes center stage in that conversation. Most of it is intangible, based on his brand name, they surmise. The brand value has been boosted significantly with the fame he acquired recently – thanks to the primetime reality show. The senior traders enter heated debates, questioning if the value of the businessman's assets have shot up to unbelievable heights as a result of his winning of the Presidency. Many argue that the documents in the brown boxes and the contents in the pitch-black iron vault may lead to a significant depression in value. There is no consensus.

The wind dies down and the conversations wither away. The President walks back to the elevator.

Further eight stories down, he walks into the dingy underground where the bank vault is. The circular heavy iron door clicks open at the touch of his fingers. Inside, on one side, are piles of green bills and gold bars stacked up. A neatly tucked folder includes the ledger that sums up the value of the stacks. He flips through the pages. The final summary is devastating; his assets barely reach the level of his father's.

60 Wall Street is not his place anymore. It is rotting from top to bottom. This is definitely not the right place to store the forthcoming haul of wealth from his Presidency. He jumps back into the elevator and retreats the path back to the mouth of the trail. The eye at the center of the masonic triangle turns red, the spark transforming to a strange mix of intrigue and alarm. It jolts him awake.

With eyes wide, he stares into the darkness. Can he create new truths in that deep underground inverted above the ceiling of his presidential bedroom? Can the undesirable truths of the trenches be bent? Can he continue to hide the true value of his wealth in the pitch-black vault until an alternate repository with significantly more fortune is established?

Outside the window, the Jackson Magnolia that gave

company to so many of his predecessors has finally lurched all the way down to the ground. Its trunk has been twisted beyond repair. The President sends a note to his secretary asking that the tree be removed immediately.

A NEW FINANCIAL SYSTEM

Another day in the Oval Office is weighed down by a torrent of litigations and allegations. The number of charges wanting to expose and prove alleged money laundering by the President when he was a businessman are only growing by the day. His attempts to utilize his immense power and authority to direct new business and profits into his real estate properties have been blocked. Well known experts in the field rule that such initiatives by a sitting president flagrantly violate established ethics rules.

It is a late summer evening. The final stretches of light from the sun that set almost an hour ago throw weak red hues on the walls of the White House. The President walks by the room of the first lady. She is fast asleep, tired from a hectic day with elementary school children she visited in ten Mid-West states. So is his youngest son in the adjoining room, with an open physics textbook on his chest. He continues to his own bedroom and settles down in the richly upholstered armchair by the window.

The noose seems to be tightening rapidly, hindering his quest to expand wealth. The haul from the Presidential Midas touch must be collected before his time in the office expires. Increasing oversight by investigators and financial gurus is alarming. They are having the reverse effect where his businesses are beginning to suffer, his net worth dwindling by a billion dollars. Time is running out. The world of wealth creation, sustenance and growth needs to be turned upside down. The validity of the current incumbent financial system must be eradicated, just like he beat the political might of established leaders to win the coveted office.

He turns off the lights, rests his head on the back cushion and shuts his eyes. His fingers gently tap and feel the carvings on the handles. Another dream begins to manifest. He welcomes this one, shutting his eyes tighter. It is about the future and the promise of a new world where wealth is acquired, stored, and grown differently.

In a modest colonial style whitewashed home in Palo Alto, California, lives a distinctly pale and intellectual introvert. The colossal campus of his company situated at one of the edges of San Francisco Bay is just fifteen minutes away.

There, pieces of hardware, software and ideas are assembled ingeniously daily by thousands of top-notch computer scientists and engineers to enhance the social media platform that influences more people than any single country on Earth. He is the CEO and owns a significant portion of the company. One can safely argue that he has substantially more power and wealth than the new Midas in the White House.

The walls and ceilings of the home feature very generous use of expensive and exquisitely grained Bocote wood beams and planks, but all painted to an even white. Most walls are lined with lace curtain windows; they make the home airy and bright with abundance of sunlight throughout the day. Designed exclusively by his doctor and immigrant Asian wife, it does not have any semblance of the immense wealth they possess. The CEO deeply cares for his wife and sometimes looks up to her as his mentor. She has been with him since his days at Harvard where he became renowned as a hacker, nerd and utterly unsocial. Now, he often worries about her because she struggles to sleep at night.

On a quiet Sunday morning, Airforce One lands in nearby Moffett Field Air Force Base. After thirty minutes, under absolute secrecy, the President appears on the white wooden doorstep of the pale CEO.

The flamboyance and warmth of the President's personality fails to win over the casual and somewhat cold welcome by the CEO. His wife tries to normalize the situation with a beaming smile and a joke about the quiet and thoughtful nature of her husband. She leads the two leaders to the large lushly landscaped backyard. The CEO assures the greatest amount of privacy for their meeting, having recently purchased the adjoining properties from his neighbors.

They sit under a pergola on beige colored outdoor sofas strewn with large colorful cushions and stuffed animals. The wife reminds them that the bright colors and demeanor of the animal toys are designed to lighten up the environment. There, the two men shake hands for the first time and begin their conversation.

The president brags about the unwavering support of his base of supporters. The base was created on social media platforms, by influencing opinions of people on a mass scale. The CEO confirms that it has been possible as a result of the fluidity of the online world, where the social media platforms operate. He boasts how his own platform shapes opinions of more than two billion people on a daily basis. The reach of his platform is far and wide. He cites an unfortunate event at a remote location in South East Asia; the influencing power of the platform is so ubiquitous that it was able to instigate instant mob behavior in a group of more than a hundred villagers. The gang lynched two young men in broad daylight and threw their severed bodies into a nearby pond. The two urban visitors had entered the rural community streets in an open top Jeep Wrangler. They allegedly flirted with two innocent village girls. It irked the villagers. The news of their flirtatious behavior spread on the social media platform like wildfire, exacerbating the careless prank to the status of gruesome rape. The CEO reassures that his engineers are hard at work to prevent such unfortunate events from happening in the future; however, he reemphasizes that the power of his platform just cannot be ignored. In the next three to four years, another two billion people will get connected, thanks to the aggressive expansion plans by his highly profitable company.

The skin above the President's thick brown eyebrows creases as with increased focus he impatiently progresses to the next topic. He reiterates he is short on time and does not want the press and media to get any wind of his visit. So, he cuts to the chase.

Truths can be created, bent and a world can be formed at will, thanks to what the CEO has created. It has been very effective in pushing forth policy agendas and deflections to the masses in a rapid fashion and when needed. There is just no way for him to apply those means to create new wealth on a viral scale and then protect it. He complains about the numerous finance and earnings-related allegations against him – that he has misused codes and regulations, inflated and deflated assets at will, and amassed wealth illegally.

Financial assets live in the physical world. They are just too easy to track and hard to maneuver around, he continues. It is impossible to change people's opinions about the measure of wealth because it is tied to cash and gold. These hard assets are tracked using ledgers that are recorded on paper or electronically in computer hard disks. In either case, such records of wealth are controlled and protected by financial institutions that are bounded by strictly enforced economic policies, taxation, and federal regulations. Electoral votes can be harnessed by changing the minds of people, he continues, but there are no methods available to collect and grow wealth the same way. Because wealth is linked to the physics and economics of the elites. What can be done to break the link?

The CEO smiles for the first time and stands up. He stretches his arms, looks around at the lush foliage. He feels the light breeze playing on his eyelashes and the slender leaves of a tall, eighty-year-old weeping willow. It was as if he knew this moment will arrive. He is about to divulge something up his sleeve. As a deep thinker, he has the knack to forecast challenges ahead of time and find opportunities to enhance his platform for more profits. With four billion individuals' minds and behaviors at his fingertips, he will soon be ready to grab the horns of the proverbial Wall Street bull and turn it upside down.

Beyond connecting the next two billion people, the social media platform will soon be extended in many other ways, he begins. His engineers are laying millions of miles of cables on ocean floors to connect the seven continents better. Fiber optic strands inside those giant cables carry all forms of communication - both voice and data – much faster and farther.

Over that enhanced platform, he will create an astounding continuum, from today's capability of influencing opinions to tomorrow's innovation - the realization and protection of new wealth. The fluidity of the online world will begin to carry the financial assets that people own. Altering individual opinions to expand voter bases and value of wealth will become synonymous on the social media platform.

The President returns an utterly confused look. The CEO takes his seat again, this time closer to the perplexed leader. He must make the concepts simpler and shorter so they can be grasped easily.

He latches on to the President's earlier comment about breaking the "link". Yes, the link can be broken, he confirms. And with it, the most powerful financial system that can support the livelihood of the entire planet will be flipped. The current backbone of American capitalism - the envy of the world - will just melt and fade away. When the link is broken, Mr. President, he continues, your net worth will begin to ride on a ledger no longer controlled by the elites or pundits.

The President leans forward, his hands clasped tightly together, and begins to imagine a plethora of new possibilities. The CEO draws him into a new world of capitalism that opens up wider and wider.

A brand-new financial system begins to emerge from the soft but assertive tone of the CEO's voice. Banks and financial bureaus lose all authority and begin to go bankrupt. All financial transactions are conducted using a new currency called Rallo, conceived and created by this genius CEO. The value of wealth owned by an entity is now stored in blockchain ledgers managed as part of the social media platform and infrastructure. As a result, the legitimacy and value of all wealth begins to be established by a mass of common people who validate or dispute each transaction. Just like opinions and votes are shaped and validated on the social media platform. This is how the "link" gets broken. His base of supporters, not the government or the financial elites, now determine his net worth. This will be the climax of his presidency - a certain and rapid realization of the Midas touch.

The President bends further forward in excitement, this time his hands reach out toward the CEO in admiration. All his wealth must be converted to the Rallo currency, he confirms. And the new wealth he amasses must be stored and grown in the online blockchain ledgers and vaults controlled and managed by the social media platform.

The CEO retreats back into the soft cushions of the sofa. He picks up a soft toy - a large dog with very long fur - places it on his lap. He cautions the President of many potential regulatory hurdles in the realization of Rallo.

The President is quick to assure that he will not leave any stones unturned to make the platform a reality. If needed, he will utilize the power of presidential executive orders. But he can only do so during his second term, when he will have less to worry about winning support of legislators or elections. He stands up and reaches out for a handshake. With the other, he signals to the secret service agent that he is ready to leave. As the President steps into the black bullet-proof Lincoln SUV, the two powerful men nod at each other one last time, a satisfied gesture of mission accomplished.

And at that very instant another realization dawns on the President. The face behind the large stuffed dog with very long fur appeared like it was made of wax. Just like his own replica is at Madame Tussauds museum. A strong breeze blows. The dog's face begins to melt and loose shape, like a patch of white cloud carelessly pasted on the deep blue California sky. He begins to emerge from his dream, a very pleasant one this time.

The sun is shining brightly through his bedroom window. A group of arborists have arrived to take down the precariously leaning Jackson Magnolia. He calls his secretary to thank her for the prompt action. He also instructs her to set up a meeting with the CEO of the world's largest social media company based in California. As he hangs up and connects his cell phone to the charger on the bedside table, he begins to contemplate his next moves that will guarantee a win for the second term of presidency.

A SURE PATH

I t is November of 2019, exactly a year before the presidential election. The nation is getting primed on all critical fronts to ensure a victory for the sitting President, to grant him another four years in office.

The elites of the country have just suffered a series of defeats. The results of their investigative efforts against the President have all fallen into deaf years. The economy is roaring. Stocks are soaring. Disloyal officials are getting ousted. And the judicial system is finally beginning to lean on his side. The path to the next term in the Oval Office seems certain. With it, the establishment of a new financial system in collaboration with the pale faced CEO from California, and the certain realization of viral wealth.

The President, with his elbows resting firmly on the Resolute Desk in the Oval office, feels supremely confident. He turns to look behind the desk and faces the portrait of his father situated next to the flag of the United States of America. He smiles at him with enormous pride. He is on the verge of exceeding the achievements of the person he has been competing against all his life. The triumphs will be on all aspects of grandeur – fame, popularity, power and most importantly, fortune that will place him at the top of the Forbes list.

In the reflection on the glass of the portrait frame, he notices his fourteen-year-old son step into the Oval Office and approach quietly. He rarely visits him, like his mother with whom he spends most of his time. The young boy is now as tall as his father. He is athletic and at school, on the behest of his mother and teachers, is inclined toward outdoor sports. His goal one day is to swim the approximately two miles from Alcatraz Island to the St. Francis Yacht Club in San Francisco in record time. And fly solo around the world on his favorite Cessna Skycatcher.

"You are almost the age when your grandfather began setting the foundations of the enormous Trump empire", he welcomes his son with a grin and points him to the chair across the Resolute Desk. The chair faces the President, with the national and presidential flags flanking him strikingly on either side. The son sinks into the leather cushion, feeling much smaller than his father. He looks away, wanting to avoid eye contact.

The expression of disinterest on the soft, handsome face irritates the President, but he hides the rising feeling. He is extremely perturbed by his son's interest in sports and the outdoors. The boy's fascination follows those of the President's eldest brother. Love for nature and flying had led the young boy's uncle – about eight years older than his father – to become a commercial pilot. Both his father and his grandfather, as his aunt tells him, considered the income from the profession highly inadequate. They equated the role of the pilot to a glorified bus driver, not worthy of the Trump name and heritage. The uncle died at his prime, aged only forty-two years, severely conflicted, frustrated, and helplessly alcoholic.

The President stands up, comes around the desk to hold his young son's soft hands. The blond-haired boy, seeing his father troubled, tries to appease. He points at the many colorful charts displayed on framed white boards mounted on the left wall of the Oval Office. He reiterates his love for economics and numbers at school and expresses the desire to understand the increasingly taller bars and upward facing arrows on the graphs.

Together, they proceed toward what the President brags as his "wall of achievements". The father begins by crowing that the country's economy is on an historic high, perhaps the greatest it's ever been. One of the fat red arrows pointing upward shows the growth in the Gross Domestic Product or GDP to 2.3%. It is nowhere near the 6% that the President campaigned on, but the young boy, then only ten years old, does not know that.

The brown and blue bars in another chart shows the progression of the Dow Jones Industrial Average, which follows the price of stocks of 30 major US companies. Thanks to his innovative initiatives related to corporate tax cuts, nationalistic policies, and promises to increase infrastructure investments significantly, this excellent indicator of the economy has reached record highs under his administration.

The next and final chart displays a mix of colorful pie charts and arrows. Unemployment is at its lowest for half a century. Since he took over the reins at the Oval Office, seven million more Americans were now on the employment roll. The colorful pies and their sizes show unemployment-related statistics for White Americans, African Americans, Hispanic Americans, and Asian Americans. Each pie has shrunk significantly since he took office.

The son inspects the charts and the three indicators of the state of the economy with great interest. He asks his father if the strong market will ensure a win for him in the upcoming election. The President smugly pats him on his back. This will help, he confirms, but the incredible practical lessons learned from his grandfather cannot be ignored. He emphasizes the importance of trusting no one and the need to surround oneself with a few staunch loyalists – both in the administration and in the judicial system. They walk back to the Resolute Desk.

For example, he continues, there are incredulous attorneys in the powerful Southern District of New York court system who are after their money. They are being removed regularly, almost on a weekly basis, to protect the Trump family's assets. Across the nation, in High and Subordinate Courts, many new conservative judges had to be appointed to support his immigration-related policies and protect the religion and ideologies of the Evangelicals. He has accomplished that at breakneck speed, nominating and appointing more than two hundred of them already.

The mention of his grandfather and his tactics once again casts a shadow of indifference in the young boy's face. At that moment, his mother arrives to pick him up on the way to a private tutor. He is relieved and departs quickly without a kiss or a goodbye.

The President leans back on the matching stained leather upholstered chair. The path to the next term in office is firmly set. Once re-elected, right at the beginning of the term, he will forcefully replace the current financial system, in accordance with his secret pact with the pale faced CEO from California. With the justice department on his side, all litigations against him will be swiftly turned null and void.

The arrows of the compasses in the instruments of the government, financial and judicial systems will be aligned to enable him to collect the largest haul of wealth ever. The President's son and heir will prepare to enroll in a business-related curriculum at one of the prestigious Ivy League colleges, this time following only his father's strict direction.

THE GLOBAL ONSLAUGHT

There is no air about her. She can pass off easily as just another working woman from a crowded and large Chinese city. But she is unique with a PhD from the renowned Montpellier University in France and a passion for virology. Her favorite expeditions away from urban life are in the caves situated in the southern, subtropical provinces of Guangdong, Guangxi, and Yunnan. In the pitch darkness of limestone crevices, she collects saliva and blood samples from bats. These nocturnal flying animals are a known reservoir of coronaviruses.

A rectangular man-made lake with green algae-ridden water barely reflects the building that stands next to it. It is a white concrete edifice with few opaque black windows. A double decker skybridge with bottle green glass walls connects it to a cylindrical gray colored structure that houses the reception and conference rooms for visitors. This is the prestigious Institute of Virology situated in the sprawling capital of a Central Chinese province. It is a biosecurity level 4 facility, the highest for biocontainment. On one evening in late December, just before the beginning of the presidential election year in the United States, mysterious patient samples arrive at one of its labs.

Moments later, the virologist's cell phone rings. She has been away a few days, attending a Biotechnology conference. The alarming news of detection of a new strain of coronavirus in patients with atypical pneumonia sends shivers down her spine. The idea of coronaviruses jumping to humans from animals in the central Chinese city seems odd. As she hops on a train back to her home city, she shudders at the thought of a possible accident in the lab she runs.

Over the next week, the virologist and her colleagues work incessantly to unlock the identity of the contagion. They remain cooped up in steel chambers for long hours, in their white protective suits inflated by blue oxygen tubes. As they successfully connect the disease to the novel coronavirus, it begins to spread like wildfire, jumping from one country to another, worldwide.

This is when the worst nightmare begins in the White House. In broad daylight this time.

With the pandemic beginning to hit cities in the East and West Coasts, the US government sets up a virus containment task force. Science and facts related to disease spread and confinement begin to take center stage in all political and social discourses. For the first time, the President is forced to yield and accept the advice of elites and grudgingly place his long and distinctly visible signature on policies based on pure science and facts. The strategy developed so ingeniously at the apartment in Cornelia street to not accept the truths of the elites begins to fall apart.

The new virus spreads rapidly across the three most populous and advanced continents, forcing collaborative containment and treatment strategies across countries. As a result, his disdain for everything global stands out as a sore thumb.

Over the next two months, the pandemic begins to cripple the economy. Businesses shut down like a row of falling cards in a domino effect, across the length and breadth of the country driving hundreds of millions to lose their livelihoods. With the economy in the doldrums, the President's chances of getting re-elected to the office begins to diminish in an alarming way. The expected haul from his Midas touch is now in severe jeopardy.

His father's black and white portrait looms large behind him as he contemplates on the Resolute Desk. Just like his father's brain latched onto the vision to get into construction surmounting challenges created by the Spanish Flu that killed his grandfather, he and his administration must now be fully absorbed in a strategy of economic revival. Businesses must be reopened rapidly to revive the economy.

The tactics of truth bending, projection and deflection are so deeply ingrained in the President's character that he decides to double down on what he has been doing all along. As if every heartbeat that gushes a new stream of blood to his brain generates a fresh new set of alternative truths to confuse and change people's opinions, in his favor.

With each new manufactured truth on social media, the advice of established doctors and virologists begin to be politicized and then deflected. Statistics related to threats of virus-spread are manipulated or ignored. The reach of scientists, doctors, and researchers to his base of voters is subdued; the scientific data they produce through intense research are either hidden or framed as fake. The President needs large televised rallies with his base of supporters to affirm the success of his policies. To lure the crowds out, the potential lethal impacts of the virus itself are minimized. Many of his supporters contract the disease while cheering him at such rallies.

The lab in Central China and its lead virologist are suddenly thrown into the center of a new attention and controversy.

China sees the trade war and related policies of the White House as threats. The Asian powerhouse therefore needs a way to retaliate. It is alleged that the government had directed the top scientists in the country to develop a new strain of virus. Once it became available, exactly fourteen months prior to the presidential election in the United States, the lethal virus was let loose from top secret research facilities. The lab in Central China is a prime suspect.

Back in the early days of the virus spread, the virologist and her colleagues had used a technique called polymerase chain reaction. They had found that samples from five of seven patients had genetic sequences present in all coronaviruses. The fire lit up by the White House administration now forces her to frantically go through her own lab's records from the past few years to check for any mishandling of experimental materials, especially during disposal. She breathes a sigh of relief when the results come back to confirm that none of the sequences matches those of the viruses her team had sampled from bat caves of the southern, subtropical provinces. While that scientific fact proves that the lethal virus was not let loose from her lab and takes a severe load off her mind, the President's fans on social media continue to wallow in conspiracies. They ignore the advice and mandates from epidemiologists as new plots from the elites to dismantle the President from the Oval Office.

The lethal disease continues to spread like wildfire where the President's denials only hold back the fire engines. More than two hundred thousand citizens perish within a span of six months. His strategy is failing; the economy continues its downward spiral. Only a vaccine can bring back his magic.

In the past, when he faced similar challenges that seemed insurmountable, he would lean on his wise political strategist. When resources within the country failed to deliver, he had made hidden pleas for help from friends and dictators in foreign countries. Can he do the same again?

The President has had a fall out with the political strategist like many of his early supporters, and they are no longer in contact. Increasingly lonelier, he becomes hell bent on repeating the same tactic. Like the original Midas, the President has become a one-trick pony.

This time he needs the help of a dictator that can force doctors and scientists in a foreign country to produce a vaccine that cures the viral disease. The vaccine must be distributed across many nations with friendly leaders who will verify its efficacy. News about the effectiveness of the treatment will be proliferated using social media. As a result, the motives of his own country's top doctors and virologists will become suspect. Their assertion that a safe vaccine can be available only after all necessary trials are completed and therefore leading to after the presidential election in November will become irrelevant.

The President's private and top-secret line to his Russian counterpart lights up on many successive late evenings. The conversations flow through unidentified strands of optical fiber inside fat cables laid on ocean floors by the pale faced CEO. Another set of favors begin to be exchanged. He is promised that a cure for the pandemic will be delivered at least a month prior to the November elections.

ANOTHER NO-FACE SYNDROME

They say that when an animal is subjected to a slow death, the body does not go through a sudden shock. The resulting meat is soft and goes a longer distance satisfying the palates of incisive foodies. Accordingly, the immigrant middle eastern restaurateur proudly serves only halal meat delicacies in his bar and hors d'oeuvre joint situated on NW 23rd Avenue in downtown Portland.

Like all others, his restaurant has been shut down to decelerate the spreading of the Covid-19 virus. Only masked patrons can be served for takeout meals. Recently, the effect of another long-standing hidden disease has been rapidly unfolding through the streets of Portland. On a pleasant June morning, he puts on his mask and steps out to join a long line of other masked individuals, to protest the killing of black people. In the distance, Mount Hood looms tall and still as usual. In its shadows, the Columbia and Willamette rivers flow gently with their usual blue and green colors absorbed from the sunny and lush surroundings. The streets however aren't the usual, with anger and frustration brewing in every intersection and sidewalk, and under the mask of each pedestrian. The subject of the resentment relates to the different shades of pigment on the human skin.

In the suburbs of Atlanta, a wild goose chase of a black jogger by two white gunmen in a truck led to his hunting down in ambush style. In Kentucky, three plainclothes policemen with no search warrant barged through an apartment door into the living room of a black couple. They fired twenty shots in execution style, killing one of them – an emergency medical technician. In both cases, the deaths were sudden. Protests erupted only locally and were subdued or abandoned quickly.

The casual and yet lethal kneeling by a white police officer on the neck of a six feet tall young black man has a different effect. Air supply to the black victim's lungs is removed gradually over a period of eight minutes and forty-six seconds. The hidden trauma of systemic racism erupts, and the fury of protesters nationwide get fed more vociferously. As if the slow and gradual death of the victim galvanized each muscle in the body of the nation to rise and make a difference. The lines of protestors are much longer, and the effects of their actions are more sustained.

The intersection of the two spreads – of the pandemic and the protests against the killing of blacks – creates a new syndrome. The splits in the society now occur in multiple dimensions and in a less apparent way.

One fracture is between those that want to stop the spread of the virus and one that brands the virus as a plot to push globalism and reestablish the power of the elites. The other divide is between a section of the society that wants to eradicate racism and the other that denies its existence and wants to protect the ever-shrinking influence and power of whites in the country.

The clashes between individuals in the factions of society increasingly become faceless. The virus spread drives one group to wear marks. The other defiant group, instead of using masks for disease protection or stopping its spread, uses them as decoys to infiltrate gatherings to create confusion and instigate violence. The people with different intentions become unidentifiable.

As local law enforcement step back and contemplate prudent steps, federal troops march in to enforce law and order. They release tear gas, scour the streets, and arrest masked individuals at random, forcing them into unmarked vehicles. The protestors and infiltrators alike are transformed to inmates with even blue striped uniforms and masks.

The widespread effects of masks and facelessness begin to blur the boundaries of society.

The one-trick pony President continues to spill propaganda daily using social media. With faces of citizens hidden, he encounters a new conundrum. In a frightening way, he is now unable to clearly identify and separate his base of supporters. At the same time, a few social media platform tzars begin to clampdown on easily identifiable falsehoods that may instigate widespread violence. For the first time, that ban includes some of his own.

EPILOGUE

As the darkness of midnight shrouds the two-hundred-year-old building on 1600 Pennsylvania Avenue NW, the President spots the ever so faint crescent moon through a French window of the south wing. On the shadowy grounds, the depressing hundred-year old Jackson Magnolia is long gone. The open space is begging to be occupied.

Another night of disturbed sleep and dreams ensues. Once again, he is pulled back through the tunnel of his ancestors. This time, the familiar wandering eye of his nightmares draws him much deeper into the crevices of time, all the way back to the year 700 BC.

The bed shakes uncontrollably, reminiscent of the onset of

an exploding orgasm with an insecure model in love with him. He experiences fits of trembling; they are rather violent. Each motion is a dizzying back and forth, like an irregularly swinging pendulum. Between a distant past in Phrygia of ancient Greece and the present in the White House. At the end of the climax, he sinks into twin tragedies of avarice across two incarnations of Midas with the golden touch.

The view from the window across the ornate reddish-brown desk in his New York City penthouse is not that of the familiar St. Thomas Church down 5th Avenue. Instead, an eagle perched on the edge of the window takes off, flying high above an arid and flat landscape on the western end of the high Anatolian plateau. He is in the kingdom of Phrygia, standing tall but unsatisfied. As King Midas.

He is the ruler of the area of the northwest where the dry steppe is crisscrossed by a river system. His subjects sport large colorful turbans to escape the blistering sun. Prominently visible veins run below the brown jagged skin of their sinewy arms and hardworking hands. They are livestock and barley farmers. Alas, significantly more profitable grapes and olive do not grow in the harsh climate. Nonetheless, Midas himself is a King with substantial wealth and lives in a grand castle. The President notices that the castle is as magnificent as his own penthouse in New York City. But, not as opulent.

On the grounds of the castle is a lush garden of white and pink roses. Midas spends hours there with his favorite daughter. Often, he tells her of his intense love for gold and desire to grow his affluence rapidly. On many occasions, she notices him cover himself with his gold coins and other things gold or the color of gold. Over time, his hair takes the color of gold.

An old schoolmaster lives in the prosperous quarters by the castle. Long and straight locks of white hair fall chaotically over his wide and wise forehead. They cover most of his wrinkled sun-burnt face but fail to diminish the prominence of his chiseled nose and chin. The king often consults with the distinctive scholar on economic policy and judicial matters.

An avid traveler, of late, the schoolmaster has been severely distressed by the state of economic disparity and status quo in the Anatolian plateau. On a stormy evening, the schoolmaster turns into a satyr and goes out of control. He is drunk with rich Greek red wine and wandering aimlessly.

When the wind subsides and there is a lull in the thundering skies, the peasants hear the schoolmaster's loud rants across the fields. They carry the tall and lean schoolmaster and place him gently on a bench in the King's rose garden. The horse's ears from the satyr's body protrude awkwardly through the white hair, as does his tail through drenched clothes covered with mud. He speaks gibberish and neighs intermittently. He is barely recognizable.

The King spends the next ten days and nights with the schoolmaster. He entertains him, but without wine. He helps him to slowly detach from the spirit and physical characteristics of the satyr. In return, the scholar delights the King and his ministers with stories and songs. The long discourses often turn into sermons about new methods of garnering power and wealth. In an eerie way, the President recognizes, the schoolmaster is like the political strategist from Los Angeles, who appeared one evening at the apartment on Cornelia Street and preached about dismantling the entrenched truths of the modern elites.

Dionysus, the god of wine, is pleased immensely at the recovery of the schoolmaster and offers the King a reward of his choice. The King, pining for fortune that multiplies rapidly, asks that whatever he touches should turn into gold. Midas is bestowed the enormous power of the golden touch.

One by one, Midas touches and transforms each rose in his garden into gold. In another vast field of social media users, an uncanny skill is similarly bestowed to the New York businessman's fingers. His ability to bend established truths and cast the elites as villains transforms the opinions of millions of voters. This is another creepy resemblance that rattles the President's back and forth delirium. The nightmare persists where the visions are interspersed by his desperate attempts to reach orgasm. Each pelvic thrust this time is returned with shriek and mocking laughter of a famous porn star.

Midas summons the peasants that struggle daily to make

ends meet by selling crops of barley. He asks them what their wish for a better life is. They unequivocally confirm their desire to convert the fields of insignificant barley to lucrative red grapes and green olives. Instead, Midas proudly leads the peasants to their respective fields and turns each barley seed into gold. One by one, the fields begin to shine blindingly with the color he has dreamed of all his life. In a parallel world, masses of people gather in large community grounds and auditoriums where the President's speeches create huge surges of support and a new movement to revive a nation.

Midas rejoices and orders a feast with his subjects. The prime rib steak, also the President's favorite, is served on an iron plate, sizzling and with scrumptious gravy on the side. The plate and its contents grow rigid and turns into solid gold the moment Midas touches it. The drink with the color and fizz of diet Coke hardens in the glass. This outcome of his enormous power and wealth is unexpected and unwelcome.

He has to hide this incredible state of starvation. His frustration results in many vilifying outbursts. In one of them, the schoolmaster is on the receiving side; the scholar decides to cut ties forever with the mad King. Lonelier by the day, Midas seeks relief from his favorite daughter. Inadvertently, he hugs her and converts her to lifeless gold. The rolling tumult continues into the parallel world where the President deflects acquisitions of adultery by likening his love and lust for young woman to his daughter.

Midas eventually realizes that the power of his golden touch is a curse. He is fragile and seeks forgiveness from the gods who give him a way out. Veiled with a mask, he limps bare feet toward the river Pactolus. He touches the clear waters and sees the power of his fingers flow out of him as the white sands turn into gold.

Redeemed of the curse, King Midas promptly returns to the rose garden to revive his daughter back to life. Next, he begins to resurrect the golden roses to their natural soft pink and white petals. The euphoria of the dream reaches a peak as the President's steadfast supporters on social media and loud rallies slowly begin to fade away. His aging pelvis struggles as the final pushes and painful moans fail to instrument the much-desired climax of love making with the sluggish and disinterested porn star.

Midas now hates wealth and splendor. He renounces his magnificent castle and moves to the countryside. The dream imagery of the parallel world curls up and then unwraps. To escape the implications of serious litigations by the Southern District of New York, the President retreats in a similar way. He too relinquishes his residency at the New York City penthouse and moves to a relatively less flamboyant home in Florida.

Once the intense desire for wealth and gold withers, Midas is at a loss with nothing to do. His one-track mind needs a diversion. He decides to learn music. His pompous attitude would not let him accept his tone deafness and severe lack of rhythm. The craving to become the greatest drives him to dissent and criticize the music of others, including that of Apollo. The gods rule that the world must not suffer from Midas' depraved pair of ears any longer. They turn his ears into those of a donkey.

The secret cannot be hidden under the thickest of turbans. Eventually, King Midas, with ass' ears, kills himself by drinking the blood of an ox.

———— ∞∞∞ ————

The faint glow of dawn wakes up the President, now leaning awkwardly in the armchair. He detests the sinking feeling that the dream leaves him with, like a bad aftertaste. He picks up the remote from the side table and turns on the TV. The pandemic continues to rage and has now affected every urban and rural corner. The social unrest against systemic racism is spreading through the streets of every metropolis in the nation. His single-minded approach focused entirely on winning the next term of presidency has caused the massive fallout. Is this his tragedy of avarice?

To escape his misfortune, the Midas of Phrygia found only one remedy, namely music. The President, on the other hand, has many cures. The idea to create another set of distractions comes immediately and most naturally to him.

He orders that a statue of himself be erected on the grounds of the White House, where the old Jackson Magnolia stood.

On Mount Rushmore, his face must be added next to President Lincoln's. They must be constructed from pure gold. In the likeness of the successful King Louis IV of Versailles, and not the failed monarch of Phrygia.

When the pale faced CEO in California begins to dilly dally and then has the audacity to remove a few of the President's posts for instigating violence, the fits of rage expressed within the walls of the Oval Office shatter all prior records. He orders his closest advisor to look at the possibility of applying the Defense Production Act to force development of an alternate social media platform. His message and propaganda must be freely delivered on the new platform, unchecked and free of the regulations and ethics of the elites. This platform must be able to operate outside the oversight of the government. After the election, the same platform will be extended to upend the current financial system. His followers and wealth will have a new home. A golden touch in that realm will endure all odds, unlike that of the original King Midas.

Like a boomerang, the distinct qualities of Midas keep returning to the President; he remains a slave of his desires. He must be in the news, constantly. The thirst for rapidly realized wealth remains insatiable. His ear for anything beyond wealth and himself remains nonexistent. Yet, using his prolific abilities to spin the traditional media and influence large cross sections of society using social media, he escapes the spiral of self-destruction.

With both hands tightfisted, the President insists that he will never be a loser like the weak Midas. Specifically, as someone who always fights back and wins in a big way, he will never drink the blood of an ox. Unless he can create another wild controversy in the media. He can fake drinking the lethal blood of an ox. Not just once but for two straight weeks and create a major debate among the elites by remaining perfectly healthy and active. Because then, besides being projected as utterly strong among his followers, he can occupy the news cycle worldwide on all forms of media. His ratings will explode through the roof for an entire month or longer leading into the presidential election.

~~ THE END ~~

CPSIA information can be obtained
at www.ICGtesting.com
Printed in the USA
BVHW081251261020
591816BV00003B/700

9 781977 234247